I0761873

TIBERIUS JULIUS ALEXANDER

TIBERIUS JULIUS ALEXANDER

~ A Historical Novel ~

DANIEL M. FRIEDENBERG

59 John Glenn Drive
Amherst, New York 14228-2119

Published 2010 by Prometheus Books

Inquiries should be addressed to
Prometheus Books
59 John Glenn Drive
Amherst, New York 14228–2119
VOICE: 716–691–0133
FAX: 716–691–0137
WWW.PROMETHEUSBOOKS.COM

14 13 12 11 10 5 4 3 2 1

Library of Congress Cataloging-in-Publication Data

Friedenberg, Daniel M.
Tiberius Julius Alexander : a historical novel / by Daniel M. Friedenberg.
p. cm.
ISBN 978–1–61614–175–2
1. Alexander, Tiberius Julius—Fiction. 2. Jews—Rome—History—Fiction. 3. Rome—History—Vespasian, 69–79—Fiction. I. Title.

PS3606 /R554T53 2010
813'.6—dc22

2010003615

I

It was about ten o'clock in the evening when, slumped in my usual worn brown leather armchair, the telephone rang. "How unusual," I thought, putting down the proofs of my new translation from the Greek of Maneto, whose early account of Egyptian history is so important. I am an old bachelor. In fact it was two years since I had retired as a director of the Chicago Oriental Institute. Who would be calling at this late hour? My only surviving niece? She was on a vacation in Israel and had no reason to call.

With the same quizzical look my two Persian cats, Alexander and Darius, twitched their tails. Alexander purred and then closed his eyes. Darius continued to look at the telephone.

"Professor Fremont? Is that Professor Fremont?"

The voice was familiar but I couldn't identify it. Then the voice changed to Greek and I realized, impossible as it seemed, it was Archbishop Demetrios, head of the *dioikein* or diocese of Deir Sant Katarin under Mt. Sinai in Egypt, actually the smallest diocese in the world. What in the name of Aristotle was he doing, calling me at this time of night?

"Professor Fremont?" the voice queried again.

"The Most Reverend Demetrios?" I asked. "His Holiness?"

"Indeed. I am calling not from Cairo, where I usually reside with my Coptic brethren, but from what you non-Greeks call Saint Catherine's Monastery. Usually nonbelievers as well, including a certain Professor Fremont."

"Epicurean, Your Excellency, Epicurean. Another type of believer." We had the same joke for thirty years. The archbishop knew I had been born a Jew but considered myself a follower of Epicurus. "Horrible," he had sniffed at my first visit to Saint Catherine's Monastery—so many years ago! But with his sense of humor he had added, "At least Epicurus was a Greek." The archbishop was fanatical about his Greek Orthodox religion, modified by common sense as when the Christian monks had to build a mosque and hospice within the monastery grounds to soothe the Egyptian Moslem authorities.

"You must come to Deir Sant Katarin," said the archbishop after some small talk. "I have to show you an astonishing find."

"As you know, Your Holiness, I am now an old man. Why me? Why not Professor Caldwell Taylor of Cambridge University? He is younger and it is summer recess at Cambridge. If it is a literary find as I suspect, Professor Taylor can also read Koinē." That was the written and spoken language from the first Cataract of the Egyptian Nile north to Macedonia, and east from Libya to Syria. It had evolved as a dialect from the Ionian Greek after the conquest of Alexander.

"I prefer you," the archbishop said. "I agree that Professor Taylor is a great scholar of ancient classical Greek, but this find is written in Koinē, which is your specialty."

"A find?" I questioned. I must admit I was flattered by his remarks. Professor Taylor and I years ago had divided the Loeb Classical Library translation from the Greek, his being the lion's share, those written by classical Greeks, while mine had been the later Alexandrians, where my knowledge of the Koinē dialect was superior.

"What is it?" I asked. At seventy-five with arthritis in my knees and elbows, I was not especially anxious to make another trip to the monastery, where I had toiled almost every summer over a period of thirty years to catalogue their extensive library's collection of ancient manuscripts.

"Do you remember, Professor Fremont, that the north wall of the monastery had been partly destroyed by an earthquake in the fourteenth century and later rebuilt? Some of the brick had fallen out of the weakened section during a recent minor earthquake and in building back the wall we found in a crevice a manuscript. Mice-gnawed, it is true, but still mainly legible. We sent it to the Hebrew University. As you know," he added with a touch of sarcasm, "you Jews are clever at that sort of thing, and they applied some scientific treatment and unrolled the scroll; actually unrolled three separate parts because some sections had not only been eaten by the mice but were rotted by time."

I held my tongue. Of course I was Jewish by birth but after years of study I had become a skeptic, or more correctly, an Epicurean. But the archbishop, no matter how sophisticated—and he was indeed—could never forget I was born a Jew.

As though to enter the conversation supporting me, my Persian cat Alexander opened his eyes and, walking to me, brushed my legs as if to say, "There, there . . . all is well."

"Why did I not call Professor Taylor?" Archbishop Demetrios answered: "It is because . . . sit down, Professor. It is a manuscript written by Philon Iudaeus! One of the monks here could read enough Koinē to see references to the man you call Philo and to believe not only is it a kind of autobiography but there are references to a Jewish revolt against Rome!"

I was stunned. As His Holiness knew, Philo was my specialty. I had translated all his known dialogues for the Loeb Classical Library and even written a philosophical analysis, which in all modesty is used as the definitive study of Philo's thought in the major universities, translated from English to French, Spanish to Italian, and even into Syriac.

That was the reason Archbishop Demetrios had called me rather than Professor Taylor. Now I understood.

I hesitated. "Is the scroll long?" I asked.

"Quite long, and there are those breaks. But with your knowledge of Philo's style, having done so many translations, you can probably put together some of the missing or faded parts."

I was tempted. "Will you pay my expenses?" I asked. "And some kind of a fee? My pension is not large."

"Yes," he said. "And you can stay with our monks in the dormitory, as you've done before. But of course we have the publication rights."

"Your Holiness, let me think about it. Can I call you back in a few days?"

"I understand. Call me at my Cairo number, which you know. I have to leave this week and will be there some time before returning to Deir Sant Katarin. And stay in good health."

"One great advantage is the dry climate," I said. "At least my arthritis will hurt less."

"Good. I wait for your call. *Theos hypsistos.* God the Most High spare you."

I got up from the armchair. The room was small. On each side of the entry door were closets for my clothes and linen. Opposite was a line of windows overlooking the grounds of the cooperative. Both sidewalls were lined with shelves holding books, old scrolls, and miscellaneous manuscripts. On one side were the Greek translations of Caldwell Taylor, those of the most prominent Greek historians, playwrights, and philosophers—the usual Plato, Aristotle, Thucydides, Aristophanes, Euripides, etc. Mingled with them were his earlier translations in which I had put slips to show errors in translation. Placed in the bottom row of shelves was a basket where my cat Darius had been trained to sleep.

On the opposite wall were the shelves that contained my translations of Alexandrian Greek literature, fewer volumes and in very limited editions—unlike Taylor, I thought to myself with chagrin and often of persons not even known to many Greek scholars. The writers were all from Alexandria by birth or choice: The great Claudius Ptolemaeus, whose original work in astronomy, mathematics, and geography places him among the geniuses of all time;

Erasistratus, who founded a school of anatomy at Alexandria and invented the catheter; and Manetho the historian, unusual for being an ethnic Egyptian.

Most of all I confess that I was the proudest of my translation of Alexandrian Jewish writers who, but for me, might have fallen into oblivion. They mainly dealt with Jewish lore and the Septuagint, the translation into Greek of the Holy Scripture. There was Demetrios, curiously the same name as the archbishop, who wrote *Kings of Judaea*, attempting to justify the contradictions of the dates of biblical events; Aristoboulos, *Explanations of the Mosaic Writ*, who in his religious enthusiasm stated that Pythagoras and Plato drew from the Pentateuch; and the amusing anonymous Alexandrian Jew who wrote a love story popular for many centuries called *Joseph and Asenath*, which tells of a beautiful pagan woman who falls in love with the biblical Joseph and their trials before a happy ending in which she converts to Judaism. On the top shelf were my translations of Philo, which had at least sold a decent number of copies.

Placed in the bottom row of these shelves, which had far more vacant space than those with the books of Caldwell Taylor, was the basket in which my cat Alexander slept. "How can I abandon all these beautiful books?" I asked myself, "if only for three or four months? It might take even longer. And where can I leave Alexander and Darius?"

As if knowing my thoughts, Alexander twitched and sneezed. He then rubbed his paws together and drifted back to sleep. He too had bad dreams, as did my hero, Alexander the Great.

I undressed after running with affection my hands over the books I had translated, got into bed, and tossed uneasily all night. It was difficult to sleep. In a furtive dream Philo came to me and said the manuscript was so unkind to his nephew Tiberius Julius Alexander, an apostate Roman general, that it would be better not to translate. Then Tiberius Alexander answered his Uncle Philo and said, "Why not? It tells a story very few know, namely that the Jewish War was a civil war as much as a war against the Romans, and if I opposed it so did many of the priestly Sadducees, the Essenes, and the Jewish nobility, including King Agrippa II and Princess Berenice, both direct descendants of Herod the Great and observant Jews. Tell the story. Translate the manuscript. Some might even consider, once the facts are known, that the Jewish War was a class war in modern economic terms."

My head was spinning. I had not been aware that Philo wrote of the Jewish War. The idea excited me. How would he analyze it differently than Josephus? And didn't he die before that great uprising started?

Three days later, after calling Archbishop Demetrios, I made flight arrangements for Cairo. A former student, Professor James Hill, successor to my chair of Classical Greek at the University of Chicago, had kindly agreed to keep my cats until my return.

II

I entered the terraced garden before Saint Catherine's Monastery. The flowers were in full bloom. The cypresses, whose low height I remembered from three decades ago, were now so high the ones closest to the monastery threw odd shadows on the near wall. I passed the charnel house filled with the bones of thousands of monks awaiting the final resurrection, in the center of which sat St. Stephen the Porter, a sixth-century monk dressed in a purple robe over his bones and holding a staff with his skeleton hand. In earlier years, first peering around to be sure that I was alone, I used to clasp the staff and say, "Hi, Stephen. Nice to see you again." Now being seventy-five and sickly, that humor escaped me and rather closer to the condition of St. Stephen I passed him with a quiet nod and not a word.

The walls of the monastery are granite, built by the Byzantine emperor Justinian in the sixth century though rebuilt several times because of earthquakes. When I first was invited to start cataloguing the library books, the front gate was closed and we had to enter hoisted to an elevated doorway by a basket pulled up. The reason, I heard, was because a distinguished German professor centuries before had "borrowed" one of the rarest Greek manuscripts and never returned it. Now, however, the gate to the entry door was unlocked because a metal detector had been installed which emitted loud buzzes if any suspicious object passed because all the books and manuscripts had been stamped with metal disks: one of several concessions the monks had made to modern technology. I was amused later to hear from my old friend Father Hieronymos, keeper of the library, that monks had made part of the collection, especially the great ikons, accessible through the internet on Saint Catherine's website. "They're ahead of me," I thought. "I still write by hand." The frightening idea passed through my mind that due to my constant research I in a certain sense lived in Alexandria in the first century of the Common Era, while these monks, inhabiting a sixth-century monastery, were half a millennium younger than I was.

Shrugging off such dark thoughts and loosening my tie, appropriately royal purple against the dark suit, I entered the Basilica of the Transfiguration, with its granite columns lit up by clerestory windows. As always, I was fascinated by the many ostrich eggs suspended from the ceiling—symbols of Christian piety because the ostrich guards with such great care its eggs. I spent at least an hour alone except for the guardian monk, also an old friend, admiring the marvelous ikons on the walls. Then I went back to the vestibule and crossed over to the library.

Father Hieronymos awaited me at the door. He bowed slightly, made the sign of the cross, and said in our mutual Greek, "Welcome"—in modern Greek because Koinē would not be clear to him. "Come with me, Professor, I want to show you that even we bend to the times." He led me to the corner in which, locked under thick glass threaded by electric wires that undoubtedly went to an alarm, was a heavy manuscript.

"The Codex Syriacus!" I exclaimed.

"Yes, our most precious possession. As you know, it was written in the fifth century and it is our most valuable manuscript." He added, "Written before the monastery was built." With awe he touched the glass top. "The Most Holy Father, Archbishop Demetrios, is making arrangements to have it brought to Cambridge University, where your colleague Professor Caldwell Taylor will have the pages microfilmed; against my wishes, I may add, but who am I to argue with our Holy Father?"

"The world indeed is encroaching even here," I thought to myself. "But like Father Hieronymos, why should I complain? We are both old, we respect too much the past, we share the same antique passion for objects soaked in the mystery of the ages, whether Orthodox Christian, Roman Catholic, Jewish, whatever, including Islamic. All scholars of the past are probably cast with that same flesh and blood." Indeed I remembered my late friend, the brilliant Hebrew scholar Professor Solomon Goitein, once told me that Arab medievalists would visit him to ask his opinion of certain Kufic phrases in the Qur'an—but only at night when they would not be seen!

The monastery collections—whose core it was rumored had been formed back in remote centuries when the secondary copies and miscellanea had been deposited for safekeeping in a predecessor pagan library by the rectors of the Great Library in Alexandria—was secondary only to the Vatican collection for its ancient scrolls. The five thousand books and three thousand manuscripts were in Greek, Coptic, Aramaic, Armenian, Hebrew, Slavic, and Georgian.

"I waste your valuable time, Professor Fremont," said my librarian friend. "Come with me." In an intimate gesture he took my elbow—the one fortunately less affected by the arthritis—and led me to a long table, or rather several long tables, abutting each other. Across them laid an extended scroll in several separate parts, about forty millimeters in height, with a total distance of somewhat less than two meters, give or take, considering the breaks between sections of the scroll. From the irregular ends of each section they were obviously not contiguous.

"Can you bring me a chair, Father?" I asked.

I examined the first scroll section. It had been rightly placed; it was indeed the start of the entire scroll. Most of the Koinē was clear; where not, my close knowledge of the language could "hop" missing letters and words to make sense of the meaning.

I bent down closer. I could not believe my eyes. I put on my eyeglasses. I could read without them but they made clearer small script.

I couldn't resist a small squeal. Father Hieronymos glanced at me to see if anything was wrong. But I could not restrain myself.

"Heureka!" I shouted, "eureka" being the same word in meaning both in modern Greek and in Koinē. The father looked at me as though I had lost my mind.

"This is not an unknown manuscript of Philo," I said with excitement. "The monk here who reads some Koinē saw the name Philo and thought it was one of his writings. But it is not. I know every one of them and it isn't even in his style. This is a scroll written by his nephew, Tiberius Julius Alexander."

"Who is that?" asked Father Hieronymos.

"Who was that? Who is that?" I exclaimed. "Tiberius Julius Alexander, born a Jew from a well-known and very rich Alexandrian Jewish family, became Roman procurator of Judaea, then praefectus of Alexandria and all Egypt, and was the top military commander of the Roman legions who destroyed Jerusalem in the Jewish War."

"Impossible!" said Father Hieronymos. "How could he then be a Jew?"

"They say he was an apostate and I suppose that in swearing to the divinity of the emperor he must have been. Of course, some Jews and later Christians did as well. The matter was debated for centuries. The writer Flavius Josephus, the closest commentator in time, wrote that 'he did not follow the customs of his ancestors,' but he never used the word 'apostate.'"

Father Hieronymos sniffed but said nothing.

I settled my eyeglasses more firmly on my nose and took from my pocket a clever magnifier with a battery-operated light, which lit up the image on which the magnification was focused. Leaning forward, I started to translate.

III

I, Tiberius Julius Alexander, sit here in my special mobile chair propped up by pillows, where I have been carried by my slaves. My large house and extensive grounds were given to me by Titus, heir to Emperor Vespasian, from an estate confiscated as property of a rich Jewish rebel crucified two years earlier by Vespasian when he swept through the Galilee. The property is on a hilltop overlooking the city of Tiberius on the shore of the Sea of Galilee, where King Agrippa II visits when not at his capital, Caesarea Philipee, but naturally he never visits me; nor of course does his sister, Princess Berenice.

Discolored patches on my skin are large. The end of my nose has dropped off; the open holes which were my nostrils drip slime. I have lost most body sensation, with ulcers on my feet while four fingers and two toes have broken off. Part of the left side of my face is paralyzed but I can still talk; and cursedly, still think clearly. Discorides, the famous Greek doctor for the Roman armies and author of the renowned *Materia Medicina*, told me four years ago I might live another seven or eight years—this disease takes long to incubate and still longer to kill.

At the start of my stay here, alone with no visitors and only ignorant slaves for company except for Isocrates, my educated Greek secretary, I ordered a mass of important book scrolls and had read to me again my studies in Greek philosophy taken while very young. But they soon bored me: philosophy from books in a certain sense is good for abstract knowledge, I thought to myself ironically, except when you need it personally. And my beloved Epicurus too had his limitations for, though it is true that we seek pleasure and avoid pain, often one man's pleasure is another man's pain. So how are we to judge objectively?

Then I turned to the Roman poets and historians. Here too I became disillusioned when I thought of my own experience on the highest level of the Roman world and my personal knowledge of the emperors of the Julio-Claudian Dynasty following Divus Augustus.

Not that what was written about them and their policies was wrong; that writing simply does not exist, though I hear from Isocrates that a noted Roman orator and political figure, Publius Cornelius Tacitus, is now writing a history of the reign of those emperors.

If so, it will be unique. Divus Augustus, the mildest of the emperors after consolidating power, exiled Ovid to a dreary outpost on the Black Sea because he wrote *Ars Amatoria*, or how to make love in three books. After that, no one dared to write on matters political or social. Horace stuck to poetry, Pliny to natural science, Seneca to philosophical essays, while Virgil was a sycophant who romanticized rural life. Only Petronius dared to describe life of the very rich at the time of Nero, who promptly commanded him to commit suicide.

In sum, except for Petronius—who tried in vain to avoid trouble by describing the excesses as committed by the newly rich rather than the old nobility—no one wrote the truth about the emperors who, aside from their disgusting personal behavior, enslaved populations and indulged in large-scale atrocities. But of course there was also another side.

It occurred to me that rather than hearing Isocrates read over and over again these classics, I might try to dictate my life to him. It would not of itself be an attack against the Roman Empire, which I felt and still feel is a civilizing force despite the many brutalities. It would simply be a true account of how it was to live on a very high level during the Julio-Claudian Dynasty and until the start of the Flavian Dynasty. And it would be as well a history of the Jews in Alexandria in the same period when something like one-third of the city was of that religious persuasion.

IV

I was told that I was born in Alexandria, Egypt, in the thirty-ninth year after Divus Augustus's conquest of Egypt at the start of his reign. This was two years before his death and the reign of Divus Tiberius.

My father was Gaius Julius Alexander, probably the richest Jew of Alexandria. He was the *alabarch*, the inspector-general for all goods coming to Egypt from the East, but of equal importance he supervised the huge realty holding in Alexandria of Antonia the Younger, Antonia Nero Drusus, of the royal Roman family and mother of the future emperor Claudius. This was an invaluable political connection.

Our second name of Julius (the *nomen gentilum*) or gens of the family had been bestowed on us by Emperor Augustus for services rendered by my father in the conquest of Egypt. This made us one of the very few Jewish Alexandrian families holding Roman citizenship and thus automatically Alexandrian citizens as well. The extraordinary exception was due to the fact that after the conquest of the Ptolemys by Augustus the Romans had reduced the position of the Egyptian Jews who spoke Greek, and hence had formerly been considered Hellenes, to the degrading status of ethnic Egyptians.

The older males of our family consisted of three brothers, my father Gaius and his two brothers, Philo and Lysimachos. Lysimachos had died in my early youth. My father had two sons, myself and my younger brother Marcus Julius. My Uncle Philo, who lived with us in our mansion, was already famous as a philosopher by the time I was a teenager. Marcus and I were thus brought up in an atmosphere both Jewish and Greek, attending the top Alexandrian academy where courses were in Greek and Latin, and listening to sophisticated conversations at home.

My first childhood memory was the daily repetition, before eating but after the blessing over the bread, of an extra phrase my father recited. It came from Deuteronomy: *Akoue, Israel! Kyrios, ho Theos hêmon, kyrios heis estin*, i.e., for those not Greek, "Hear, O Israel! The Lord our God is one Lord." Later I came to realize that as a pious Jew living among pagans with their many gods, my father wanted to impress on my brother Marcus and me at a very early age the unique Yahweh of our religion.

The second memory is also religious. Every Sabbath eve we went to the *proseuche*, our house of prayer being the Great Basilica of Alexandria, renowned—and not only by Jews but also by pagans—as a world-famous structure. It was said to hold one hundred thousand persons, an enormous long building with double interior columns to support the beamed roof. The *proseuche* was located in the Delta district, where most of the Jews lived, close to the water for ritual baths.

There were seventy gold chairs (oddly, one Friday evening, when bored with the service, I counted seventy-one) where the revered elders sat, including my father and Uncle Philo. I may add that much later my father told me the chairs were gilded and not gold, otherwise the Alexandrian Greeks would have long since stolen them.

At the front of the *proseuche* was a marble throne, the Seat of Moses, flanked by two roaring stone lions that terrified me as a child. In the middle of the building was a wood platform from which the triennial cycle of the reading of the Torah was conducted, the prayers being directed to *Theos megalos*, our Greek for Great God. The minister stood on the platform and the basilica interior was so long that when someone went up for the reading a scarf was waved so the congregation could recite "Amen." The interior walls were covered with votive shields dedicated to the emperors by the loyal Jewish Alexandrians. The floor was paved with colorful mosaics, different panels showing peacocks and grapes—ancient signs of fertility—and menorahs, shofars, and lulavs, sacred Jewish cult objects.

On a raised platform of the basilica stood an ornate marble base on which rested the Ark holding the scrolls of the Torah. Enclosing the platform was a marble chancel screen fitted to movable posts. The window grilles bore a pattern of an intricate double meander with stylized rosettes. At the main entrance, carved into the marble and highlighted in red paint, were gold-leaf inscriptions showing the names of donors with a description of their donations, ending with a blessing.

In the center of each of the two sides of the basilica were doors, one leading to the *exedra*, or meeting hall, to study the Torah, the other to the assembly room for community events, called *synagoga* from the Greek word "congregation."

As a child I was fascinated by these Sabbath services. The nearest chairs to the seat of Moses were occupied on one side by my father and on the other by my Uncle Philo, the two most distinguished Jews of Alexandria. Due to the great many contributions made by my family—including, as was widely known, my father's gift of the gold and silver plating over the inner doors of the Holy Temple in Jerusalem—as a special dispensation my father's two boys, I and my brother Marcus, were allowed to sit on purple silk cushions before the chair of our father.

When very young I was docile and quiet during the Sabbath service. Its repetition every three years then began to weary me. Unlike my brother Marcus, who was a paragon of patience, I became bored. It all seemed so long and far away. I also became intrigued. Why wouldn't Yahweh, if He was all-knowing, find Adam in the Garden of Eden? If Adam and Eve were the only two human beings, where did the rest of us come from? And wasn't it wrong for the daughters of Lot to get their father drunk to sleep with him, though I wasn't sure what that meant.

At home, when I asked such questions, my father, a pious Jew, would flush with anger and order me up to my bedroom. What made it more difficult was that my brother Marcus never questioned a religious text or anything else for that matter; and what was worse was that my brother Marcus was so handsome, taking after my beautiful mother, while I resembled my father, with a thin face, dark skin, a hooked nose, and so hairy that later I had to scrape my face with pumice stone twice a day to avoid looking like a barbarian.

My sole consolation was my uncle, who smiled and tried to answer my questions. To Philo everything was allegorical and thus a higher truth than facts. He was just as religious a Jew as was my father, but more open. The people who appeared in Genesis were simply allegories of states of the soul; and furthermore, he declared that the Greek philosophers such as Aristotle and Plato had drawn from Moses everything good since the Pentateuch contained all truth. To my uncle, the body was a prison for the soul which sought to rise again to Yahweh. Thus, to amplify his view, when Yahweh pretended not to know where Adam was in the Garden of Eden, that was simply expressing that man, i.e., Adam, should always seek Yahweh. The expulsion of Adam and Eve was only symbolic of the need to avoid temptation; and their other children were never mentioned because they were not pertinent to the story. As to Lot and his daughters, the point was twofold: avoid drunkenness and practice vigilance over daughters.

These explanations did not satisfy me but at least they were better than the rage of my father at my impudence, especially when compared to the pleasing behavior of my brother Marcus. So as time went by, I became more attached to my Uncle Philo and resolved, unlike Marcus, to avoid, if possible, entering the family business where my father would dominate me.

The other sharp memory of my early youth—I believe I was about four—occurred long before I started to question the religious practices. It was the funeral service for Lysimachos, my father's other brother. From his life to his death had only been a week and not one of the famous Greek doctors was of any help. In fact, Lysimachos's death was among the many thousands that year in one of the plagues that periodically struck Egypt as described in the story of Moses.

At the death ceremony my mother, clutching me with one hand and Marcus with the other, continually wept. I was not aware at the time but it was the first break in our tightly knit family, which, as I will relate, dissolved in my life span. Such is the destiny of mankind—even in my days the Julio-Claudian Dynasty, which had seemed eternal, disappeared to be replaced by the Flavian Dynasty. But my part in that change I will come to later.

V

I don't recall exactly how old I was but since it was twelve years into the principate of Emperor Tiberius and shortly after I was called to the Torah, I must have been fourteen when my father asked me how I was doing in my study of Latin at the Arista academy of Alexandria, where the Aristotelian disciplines such as logic, rhetoric, and metaphysics were taught in Latin as well as Greek. I replied evasively, not telling my father of the taunts I received daily from the other students as a Jew.

"Can you understand normal conversation in Latin?"

"I think so," I said.

"You are now a man," my father replied. "It is time for you to know more of the world and specifically more of our family business. All you seem to do is study philosophy like your uncle and read military history at the Great Library."

"And Marcus?" I asked.

"Let's not worry about Marcus," my father said stiffly. "He has a good practical head on his shoulders. He's already helping out with the books at our Canopus warehouses."

I said nothing.

"You have of course heard of Nikanor and Sons when we talk at the table," said father.

"Yes, it's some kind of business in which the family's involved."

"More than involved. We own the firm despite the Greek name. As inspector-general of all imports coming from the East into

Alexandria, I also do business directly with the Arabian countries and those even farther—such as ivory, spices, pearls, precious stones, and silk coming from as far away as India and China. But today we are not going to visit our warehouses at Koptos in the Thebaid." I knew the Thebaid was the southernmost of the three divisions of Roman Egypt.

"Where are we going then?" I asked, having little interest in seeing stockpiles of precious commodities guarded by the Nubian employees of my father.

"We are going to meet the commander of the 5th legion stationed in Egypt. There are two, the 5th and the 10th, but I have a special reason to see the commander of the 5th, who controls the Egyptian south. Incidentally, like most Romans, he has contempt for Egyptians, Jews, and Greeks, so watch your tongue and be respectful."

"I don't want to go," I said. "Besides, my Latin isn't good enough."

"I didn't ask whether you wanted to go," my father said severely. "I said you were going. I want to see if you can follow the Latin taught to you at the academy. It cost me enough. You may have business with Rome someday."

The trip on the Nile was uneventful. The 5th legion was stationed at Elephantine, above the first Cataract, to guard against invasion from the south: actually, as I learned later, to set the stage for a possible invasion of Ethiopia, reputed to be a land of great gold deposits. The commander, Lucius Trisasea Sabinus, of noble birth, had been informed of our arrival.

"Welcome, Gaius Julius." He extended his hand, emphasizing the noble name of Julius. "Welcome to this lonely outpost."

I looked around curiously. The legionnaire camp was a large square closed in by a high wood fence. On the walled fence spaced at equal distances were towers, and crowning the towers were holes for shooting arrows as well as slinging stones. In a special space behind the wall, I could see several battering rams, vast beams of wood with their heads covered by a thick rib of iron. Thrust forward, these rams could batter walls, breaking down the thickest. The tents of the centurions, the officers over one hundred men, were in the middle of the camp, in the center of which one could see the praetorium, the commander's lodging. Surrounding the fence, which enclosed the camp, was a large deep trench.

What impressed me more than the fort with its six thousand legionnaires, as I had been told was the usual size of a legion, was the courtesy shown by everyone to my father. In Alexandria he surely did evoke respect among the Jews, being the individual responsible for their good behavior and conduct to the Roman *praefectus*, or governor, but here it would have seemed different.

It was apparent that the legion commander, Lucius Trisasea Sabinus, wanted a private conversation because he dismissed the officers and sat across the table from my father as though the two were equals.

"I understand there has been no trouble with the shipments of late," the commander said with a smile. "My legionnaires are doing a good job."

"They are indeed," said my father. He took out a wad of papyrus marked with numbers. "The total is better than usual."

"Thanks to Jupiter," said the commander, "I have only a little more money to pay for my villa at Pompeii though I still have two more years to go before my twenty-five years of service are up, most of it in this infernal climate that is only fit for Egyptians, a wretched race."

"Have there been any casualties at the Nile outposts?" my father asked. "Someone told me there was a serious skirmish with Arab brigands."

"No. An exaggeration. The Nile ran shallow this year and a group of starving fellaheen tried to steal some of the supplies at Heptakomia. Following instructions, my soldiers killed them all and left their bodies for the hyenas."

"Good." My father beamed. "Here are the receipts." He handed the package of papyrus sheets to the commander. "And here is the money. You need not count it now. The sum is correct. You know me all these years. Not a drachma short."

The Roman commander smiled. He shook the moneybag, which jingled. "What a pleasant sound," he said.

"And well worth it for both of us," my father added. The two men clasped hands with affection.

"Can I give you a guard to go back to Koptos?" Lucius Trisasea Sabinus asked.

"No," my father said. "We are going straight back to Alexandria. Besides, I brought some Nubians with me. They are trustworthy." He laughed. "And now especially since it is you who has all the money."

The commander walked us to the main gate, a signal honor which his legionnaires watched with curiosity.

"Six months?" asked my father, "November?"

"Can you make it sooner?" asked the commander.

"Then let's make it late September. But give me a while to collect from the Hellenes in these troubled times," my father said. "With all the tension in Alexandria between the Greeks and the Jews, business is slumping."

"All right. But no later. Each day of my last two years in this climate of Inferno seems like a decade in my hometown of Pescara. The gods be with you."

"Equally be with you," said my father. And the two men smiled.

As we traveled north on the Nile my father lapsed into silence. Knowing his nature, I too remained silent.

"Tiberius, don't you want to know why I took this trip and why I asked you to come?" he finally said.

"Why?" I asked.

"My son," my father said, "I wanted to open a little curtain for you on the real world. I know already—I've spoken to your teachers at the academy—that you are very smart and can speak and understand Latin well. Indeed, my brother Philo goes further. He says you're not only smart but too much of a freethinker. While

Philo regards the truth of our religion as expressed in allegories, similar to the allegories of the Greeks who indeed took them from us, he thinks you seem to feel both may be false and that we humans might have invented Yahweh out of fear or ignorance: he claims you once said the only sure truth is that man seeks pleasure and power. Is that true?"

I was scared. I didn't know what to say. My uncle and I were preparing several dialogues where I might, contrary to him, take that view. But how could my father understand?

"I'm not sure what I think," I said lamely. "But you haven't told me why I was invited to see the commander of the 5th legion with you."

"I think you are now old enough to understand. I am inspector-general for all goods coming from the East, a very profitable position. I owe it to two things, which I will explain. In Augustus's conquest of Egypt he had assembled a huge army to defeat Marcus Antonius and Queen Cleopatra, drawing them from Gallia, Hispania, and Germania, as well as his own Roman troops. The cost was enormous; even Maecenas, the richest Roman and great supporter of the future emperor, was strained for money. It was then I, though very young, anticipated his victory and went to my rich Jewish friends and raised a large sum to support his army.

"As everyone knows, Octavius, later Emperor Augustus, never forgot a friend. He graciously allowed me to adopt the cognomen of Julius for my services, also granting me Roman citizenship. And the second thing is that he persuaded Antonia the Younger of the royal family and mother to Claudius, to hire me to manage her large realty holdings in Alexandria. This is why no Roman praefectus of Egypt has dared to deprive me of my position as *alabarch*; and indeed my wife Rachel, your mother, and Antonia are close friends.

"The one thing I couldn't do is to break the Alexandrian Greek monopoly over the many kilometers of docks along the waterfront, a consortium with links to top Roman aristocrats. They have an arrangement which permits the Greek oligarchs to charge outrageous fees for docking privileges.

"So, Tiberius, I thought up an idea. Those oligarchs don't of course control the roads leading into Alexandria through the desert parallel to the Nile. What I did is make a similar arrangement with the commander of the 5th legion stationed to guard the south of Egypt. We built a port near Koptos to which we have our commodities shipped from the East. The commander you met, then in the name of security, had his legionnaires erect a series of blockhouses every several thousand meters along the Nile, stationing them at each post.

"My goods now flow freely to Alexandria by land, where they are transferred to our Canopus warehouses, bypassing the docks. And my friend, Commander Lucius Trisasea Sabinus, receives a five percent commission on the profits. Since the docking charges on the waterfront controlled by the Greeks are ten percent, we both came out ahead. Koptos is where we receive the spices, glassware, and fine textiles from Syria, the perfumes and spices from Arabia, and precious gems and silks from as far away as India and China. Because there are so many different countries evolved, we have our own money changers who for a small commission work with us to facilitate the transactions."

I was astounded. For one thing, I had never heard my father talk to me for so long in all my life. For another, I had always thought the Romans were honest and would prohibit a legion commander from taking money in such a scheme.

"But isn't that dishonest?" I said in my naiveté.

My father flushed. "Don't talk to your father that way. Dishonest! What is dishonest about avoiding the Greek dockside monopoly? What is dishonest about setting up security stations along the Nile to protect traffic? How dare you say that to me!"

Curiously, listening to my father, a very pious Jew, I thought of some of the Greek philosophers who taught at my academy and who could turn a nail into a hammer and a hammer back into a nail with very logical arguments. Was my father's thinking much different? That was an important moment in my life. For one thing, I found the Roman 5th legion far more interesting than the Jewish basilica I was forced to attend every Friday dusk. For another, I decided to study and see if there was or was not an allegorical meaning, as my Uncle Philo insisted, deriving the Greek religion from ours. A few kilometers from our mansion was the ideal place to find out. It was the Great Library at Alexandria, the greatest library in the world.

VI

The Great Library was an important part of Alexandria, the second-largest city of the Roman Empire. It was the city where I was born, attended Torah studies when very young, was called to the Torah, and graduated from Arista, the most famous of Greek academies. Alexandria was the safest all-weather harbor along the Great Sea's northern coast of Africa and western coast of Asia. Into its long docks, extending down to Canopus, sailed ships carrying the precious goods of the Orient. The city was also famous for its manufacturing: linens, carpets, tapestries, glassware, and perfumes. It was almost the sole source of papyrus, for which it supplied the empire. In sum, Alexandria was the emporium, the market for the whole world.

The two corsos, the main boulevards, were never quiet, day or night, always humming with the sound of chariots and commercial vehicles. In the huge central park could be seen the gigantic palace of the ancient kings and queens, the famous museum (actually a university), the Great Library, the shrine of Osiris, the most popular Egyptian god, and nearby, the mausoleum with the crystal coffin holding the preserved body of Alexander the Great. As a boy and adolescent I had viewed all these places with wonder and also bet at the Hippodrome, the racetrack. Several times I had walked across the bridge, the *Heptastadium*, which connected the mainland to the Isle of Pharos with its famous lighthouse, forty stories high; the whole coastland to Canopus was one extended luxurious yacht basin with restaurants and bathing beaches.

What I wanted, however, was not the pleasures of Alexandria but rather its accumulated knowledge. Like the Roman families of the ruling class who preferred to consult doctors who had studied anatomy in Alexandrian medical schools, I looked to the Great Library for what I sought, mainly the meaning of religion. There were nine hundred clerks working there, with some 750,000 scrolls of papyrus representing all known languages and literatures. But I had no problem finding the scrolls I wanted because the chief librarian was a close friend of my Uncle Philo, and probably more important, my father made it a point every year to give the library large sums of money "in the name of the Jewish community." In fact, the clerks made available a private room for my research, which I did daily after attending my studies at the academy.

What I found confirmed my doubts. There was no true religion. Wherever one was born, in whatever group, there one learned from childhood and believed in the religion of that group. Even in mixed societies, which had begun to form in the major cities of the Roman Empire, each subgroup followed the religion of its elders. And the ways they were similar and dissimilar surprised me. To show my Uncle Philo, who insisted that they were all of the same true belief in the soul and in Yahweh—and most times he was correct—I created a simple review of the major beliefs.

I did not bother including the Greek and Roman regions, with their pantheons of gods and goddesses, all of which my Uncle Philo knew and indeed wrote about. What had always amazed me was the attitude of contemporary Greeks everywhere, but especially a source of friction in Alexandria, who called the Jews atheists because they permitted no statues in their sanctuaries. This shocked the Greeks since they claimed that the Jews did not believe in the gods. Indeed, as I learned soon enough, this led to riots and many deaths when the Hellenes, to please Emperor Caligula, pointed out they could not put statues of Augustus—now considered Divus or a god—in any place of Jewish worship.

But the conception of Yahweh varied less than I had thought the more I studied. The different religions had many things in common. Almost all believed in resurrection in one form or another, excepting the Jews who, divided as usual, had the Pharisees, the largest group, believe in a kind of existence after death, while the Sadducees, the priests and the aristocrats, did not. Elsewhere it was almost universal. In Syria the resurrection of their god Tammuz was greeted with the cry "Adonis [another name of the god] is risen," and celebrated at the close of his festivals. This was similar to the Greek ritual which hailed the agony, death, and resurrection of Dionysus. And the worship of the great mother Cybele in Lydia and Phrygia, which spread to Africa and to Italy, centered around the death of her beloved fellow god Attis. Her priests drank their own blood and then bore in procession the young dead god to his grave. The next day the people exalted as the priests cried out that Attis was resurrected, the god was saved and for his followers would come salvation. Indeed, in Rome the image of the Great Mother Cybele was carried in triumph through the streets as *Nostra Domina*, Our Lady.

In the Zoroastrian creed all history and life were represented as a war between the holy forces of life and the diabolic forces of darkness; in the end a savior, Mithras, would come to judge all human beings and establish an everlasting reign of righteousness and peace. Mithras was then called to heaven after celebrating a sacramental last supper.

Even more widely honored was the cult of the Egyptian goddess Isis, the mother, the comforter, the bearer of eternal life. Her great spouse Osiris had died and risen from the dead; the happy resurrection was celebrated throughout much of the Mediterranean with great ceremony. Isis was represented in pictures and statues as holding her divine child Horus in her arms, and devoted liturgy hailed her as Queen of Heaven and mother of God.

These religions all seemed to spring from Asia or North Africa. Their beliefs obviously represented a common set of religious values, as my Uncle Philo grasped. However, when it came to the spiritual values springing from the greatest minds of classical

Graecia, half a millennium earlier, there was a complete contrast. Of course the masses of Hellenes had their Bacchic and Orphic rites, but among the educated and more thoughtful Greeks, especially the Ionians, there arose skeptic and cynic schools which questioned the blind belief of the common people and searched for other truths. The greatest, Aristotle, wrote that there might indeed be one god or several gods; but he was certain that they took no interest in mankind. These Uncle Philo ignored; these I found more attractive, especially when compared with the monotonous repetition of the Jewish Septuagint as holy dogma.

With the reluctant approval of my father, who had given up hope of a commercial trade for me and was training instead my brother Marcus, a more pliant son, I decided to debate my uncle in several written dialogues. My extensive study had convinced me that organized religion was a dupe based on the fears of mankind—and perhaps a good business for the priestly castes—or more probably a combination of the two. Philo was already famous for his writings and, as I look back, my arrogance was unbelievable. But my uncle consented. I only participated in a few written and minor debates. They were *De animalibus*, as to whether animals had real intelligence, and *De providentia*, the latter which had two parts. In the second, in both parts I refuted providence as the benevolent guide of Yahweh, pointing out that many wicked people were prosperous while many good people not, citing historic examples. My uncle responded in a manner which I could not accept, emphasizing the unimportance of earthly values. If the good are punished in the world and the evil rewarded, I asked, what is providence? My father insisted that the evil eventually pay. I still remember a startling example which he used: "Like a ship which dances in the open seas is incapable of steering and progressing, but inclines sometimes to one side and sometimes to the other, and pitches, thus the wicked person having a wayward and agitated spirit, incapable of directing proper steering, is always carried by his cares toward his own destruction."

Though so long ago, I recall at that point I felt like reminding my uncle of the women and children murdered by the Romans at Carthage and the million slaves taken by Julius Caesar after the Gallic War, or even the fate of the Gracchi brothers who tried to save Rome from tyranny—but at my young age I felt it wise not to bring up such examples.

What I considered better in my attempted refutation was the case of Socrates, who though of like opinion to that of my uncle, was condemned to death. Philo's answer, I must admit, I also found unconvincing. He claimed that no earthly splendor ranks in Yahweh's sight as a good, so therefore wise men despise all the vain thoughts and values of idle opinion but, like Socrates, consider there is nothing good or excellent save in acquiring virtue. This to me was avoiding my question.

A friend of my father had a slave who recently tried to escape. He was caught and put to a painful death. In Rome I knew that when a slave attacked his master not only he but, as an example, all the slaves of the master were crucified. How, I was about to ask, did that accord with his view of Yahweh's providence? But I felt it wiser to stay silent. My uncle, as did all the rich slaveholders, believed in that institution. I was also tempted to ask Uncle Philo, who did nothing in the sense of usual work but lived on our family fortune, how he would feel—and if he would still hold the same philosophy—were he a slave himself. But of course one does not say such things to such a revered man. And perhaps, I thought, maybe I was too immature to grasp the deeper truth. I will say however that my uncle flattered me by stating that my retorts were those of a *sapientiae amator*, a lover of knowledge, and even dedicated his long essay *De aeternitate mundi*, or the Eternity of the World, to me.

Notwithstanding that my father had given up on me as a businessman, my uncle, still hoping to convince me that my religious skepticism was wrong, took me to two different meetings. The first was a visit to a colony living on nearby freshwater Lake Mareotis. Philo had heard this group largely shared his philosophy. They were called *Therapeutae*, or Worshipers, and were spiritually related to a small similar group in and near Jerusalem called the Essenes. This was his first visit. The lake was within walking distance of the city and actually set its northern boundary.

It was a disappointing experience for me, whose vision of life had become wholly material. This sect of ascetics was far more disciplined in their mode of life than the Jews of Alexandria, many of whom my father—and among them were some of the richest friends—had once sarcastically called "Jews only on the New Year and Day of Atonement." The Therapeutae scorned money and sex, lived separately one from the other though gathered for worship, and devoted their lives to meditation and prayer.

The community center was built on a low hill at the edge of the lake, each person having a separate cabin in which the person studied sacred literature. They had given away their wealth and were opposed to slavery as well. My uncle noted their customs and later actually wrote a dialogue about them called *De vita contemplative*. He was fascinated. I was not. Though still a rather young adolescent I was already familiar with the street where were located the best brothels of Alexandria and I preferred warm living flesh to litany praising the long dead.

The second visit was more interesting. Uncle Philo explained that there was a new peculiar branch of Judaism which had just been established and rather mysteriously was spreading not only among the Jews but in the pagan world as well. Its founder was a certain Yeshua who preached in the Galilee and, moving to Jerusalem, had attacked the money changers at the Holy Temple. Indeed, he scorned making money itself as a form of sin, and then—so it was said—had proclaimed himself, though indirectly, as the long-sought-for Messiah.

We entered a shabby room in the poorest area of the Delta, the district where most of the Jews lived. The room was filled with perhaps twenty or twenty-five laborers of the lowest class, dirty and unkempt, some with their wives who sat behind a thin gauze curtain.

The leader, if so he may be called, was a middle-aged swarthy man with deformed hands, but he did not need assistance in reading the required section of the Septuagint for that Friday night because he knew it from memory. His Greek was bad; he was obviously a foreigner, probably from Judaea.

During the service, which was entirely correct except for the repeated references to Christos, the Greek word for Messiah, as though to a Divus, as well as to a certain Miriam, presumably the mother of Christos. The mixture of these names with the standard Jewish service confused me. I glanced at my uncle and noticed an ironic twist to his lips. What really startled both of us, however, was that at the end of the service the audience lined up before the speaker, who took from a box unleavened bread and poured into a small cup red wine from a flask, and each of the listeners ate a morsel of the bread and sipped from the cup of red wine. Then, without glancing at us, they left.

My uncle went up to the leader. "Yahweh be with you," he said. "My name is Philo, Philo of Alexandria. Perhaps you've heard of me."

"What Jew hasn't!" exclaimed the speaker. "I am Marcus, usually called Mark, recently come to Alexandria. I am a bishop of the Yeshuites. Yeshua, as you surely know, is Jesous in Greek and Jesus in Latin."

"This is my nephew, Tiberius. We have come to witness your extraordinary ceremony. Are you Jews?"

"Of course. What else?" responded Mark with astonishment. "We are Jewish followers of the *Messias*, the Anointed, who finally came to fulfill the ancient prophesy of one who would turn the entire world to truth, charity, and humility, following Yahweh's commands. For that he was crucified and ascended to heaven."

"Crucified! That can't be," my uncle exclaimed. "By Roman law only slaves and traitors are crucified."

"Yet he was crucified to atone for man's sins and lead mankind to justice and eternal peace. His sacrifice was not that of bulls or goats but that of his own flesh and blood."

My uncle threw a sidelong glance at me as though to say be

patient with a fool and then asked, "How do you know he was the *Messias*?"

"In preaching it was apparent, and his followers knew this to be true by his healing the sick and raising the dead."

"He sounds more like a magician," I said, speaking for the first time.

"Yes, a magician sent by Yahweh to perform miraculous works and show mankind the path to salvation."

"And who vouches for that?" asked my uncle.

"The heavens themselves proclaim it." Mark raised his eyes. "Yahweh sent his only son to redeem mankind and by his crucifixion to atone for their sins. He was buried but in three days ascended to heaven, Yahweh be blessed. If you believe in Him, the true *Messias*, Christos in your Greek language, you will be saved." Mark made the sign of a cross on his chest. "And that I know is the way to truth and the path to salvation."

"And what is that sign made on your chest?"

"That," said Mark, "is the sign of the cross, of the crucifixion, the sign of redemption through his sacrifice."

At this point my uncle abruptly turned and left the room. I followed. "What a madman," he said. "What a perversion of our holy religion. And the idea of a crucified deity is absurd."

"And yet uncle," I said, "at the end of his reading in his little speech before the congregation left, he said things that reminded me of your writings. In your dialogue, on the life of Moses, *De vita Mosis*, which I recently read, you wrote of Moses as the ideal king linking the people with the spiritual order; and at the end you wrote that belief in Moses and the Torah freed men from death when their souls would return to the immaterial, the highest form of eternal life. Substituting their Yeshua for Moses, or perhaps supplementing Moses with Yeshua, and his thinking sounds much like yours."

I had never seen my uncle angry but this time he was. "How dare you, Tiberius, compare their Yeshua, who sounds like a fraud or false prophet, to Moses! Why I believe these so-called Jews are pagans. Yahweh is One. Yahweh is not two or more, like those ridiculous Greek or Roman deities. To think, to believe he had a son is obscene, is paganism. And notice that ceremony at the end, obviously a metaphor for drinking blood and eating flesh of their Christos. What could be more blasphemous for a Jew than drinking human blood and eating human flesh, even if only in metaphor? This disgusting perversion of Judaism cannot last. It is straight out of paganism. It is like the worshiping of Zarathustra, who indeed said many centuries ago, as I recall, 'He who eats of my body and drinks of my blood, he shall know salvation.' This new perversion cannot last. It is mishmash. Why, for all I know, they might even give up circumcision, Yahweh's covenant with Abraham."

I laughed at this ridiculous thought.

VII

Then came the major crossroad in my life.

I had been spending almost every afternoon after my studies at the academy in the Great Library on the Canopus Way when I stumbled into someone going up the steps as I left.

"Pardon me," I said, not looking.

"Pardon me," a young woman's voice answered.

I was startled and glanced up, for no women were admitted into the library.

There are moments in life which are frozen in the mind and have no relation to what we call time. Time is considered the point shown by the shadow on a sundial. A Greek philosopher—I forget which—said time was not objective but rather related to human experience: the future is hope, the present sensation, the past memory. Contrary to that philosopher, the meeting on the steps of the library was forever for me.

The girl—she was not really a woman—was about my height, neither tall nor short. She had white skin that was bronzed to a golden tint by the hot sun of Alexandria, while flaxen hair, without curls, fell to her shoulders. Her eyes were emeralds, flawless emeralds, as I knew because my father owned one of the few emerald mines in Egypt, near Aswan in the south, and from childhood, I had been shown the difference between a merely good emerald and a flawless emerald. Her nose was short and straight, with a small mole on the left nostril. She wore white pearls set in silver earrings. Her fingers were exceptionally long, without rings, the nails painted green to match her eyes. Open-end white sandals showed toenails also painted green. A slender body, her small breasts bobbed under her silken olive dress as she moved. With painted lips a bright rose color, there was a piquant and sensual scent to her body caused by the late Egyptian sun. I saw and felt all that in a flash. I see all that again and again through all my life. I see and scent that now as I sit in my mobile chair with long arms and a foot support, a very sick old man, where I view the Sea of Galilee. That moment was the golden moment of my life, never to be surpassed; that moment has stayed longer in my mind, and recurs more than whole decades that have slid into nothing.

I stuttered. I was overwhelmed as only a young man of no experience in real love can be, almost paralyzed.

"My name is Penelope," she said, smiling. With female intuition she knew she had made a conquest. "Penelope Timoclea," she added.

"Tiberius Julius Alexander," I said.

"Alexander . . . Alexander . . . you don't look Greek."

"A Jew," I said abruptly, terrified that she would walk away.

"Any relation to Philo Alexander, the philosopher?" she asked.

"My uncle."

"What an honor to meet you," she said. "My father is a librarian and that is the reason I've come here. Otherwise they wouldn't admit a woman. My father has great respect for your uncle. He thinks he's the most important living philosopher in Alexandria. We are of direct Macedonian descent; our family—the first was a soldier in Alexander's army—came to Egypt with Ptolemy I Soter and we've stayed here, though still Macedonian Greeks. But unlike many of the Greeks, we respect your people. I have no negative feeling, following my father, about the Jews."

I looked at Penelope. Then an odd thought came to my mind. I wanted to *eat* her. I wanted to take her not only as a woman but as a part of me. I could almost taste her. Were my father and uncle right? Did we have souls? Was that one way of thinking of the soul? And then I thought of Plato's *Symposium*, which I had recently studied at the academy, where he wrote that man and woman were artificially separated and thus longed to become one together again.

"Which way are you walking?" I asked.

"As I said, I must meet my father now. But tomorrow, if you like, we can meet at this time at the corner of Soma and Canopus, at the square containing Alexander's tomb."

"Agreed," I said, sweating. Would she come? Would a descendant of Ptolemy's Macedonian troops, Greeks who usually hated us, actually come? I spent the whole night trembling. She aroused me so strongly that I relieved myself two times during the night. And still the desire remained.

Next afternoon Penelope was there. She chatted intimately as though we were old friends. We entered the chamber holding the royal sarcophagus and looked reverently at the body of Alexander in the crystal coffin set in gold. I told Penelope—which I could see she thought might not be true—that Ptolemy I Soter, or Savior, had seized the conqueror's corpse by force of arms as it was being brought from Babylon to Macedonia in order to ensure the legitimacy of his rule over Egypt, and then he had moved the capital from Memphis to Alexandria, where he built the magnificent tomb holding the mummy of Alexander.

Penelope then pointed to the mummy's broken nose and I explained that Octavius, the future Emperor Augustus, opened the case to put a golden crown on the head and that the crown slipped and broke Alexander's nose. As a Macedonian by heritage, she sniffed scornfully while I told the story. I then saw she was no lover of the Romans, common enough among the Greeks who had been despoiled of Egypt by Augustus.

We met every afternoon. There was small chance of our being discovered together. In a city of about one million people, Alexandria was surrounded by wall or sea and even in the main streets—the city is built on a narrow strip of land between the Great Sea and

Lake Mareotis—there were really only two thoroughfares of importance. One was the Canopus Way, east-west, some eight kilometers long. The other was the Street of the Soma ("Soma" or "Body," referring to the tomb of Alexander), north-south, about the same width but a smaller distance. The side streets were laid out parallel to those main boulevards and they were all so packed with pedestrians or men on horse-drawn chariots that meeting a familiar face was remote.

We explored the city together, the difference between Jew and Greek totally forgotten in our mutual pleasure. Penelope was sixteen, I a bit older, but under the Egyptian sun boys and girls ripen into men and women early, and as they ripen so do their desires. I was obsessed with Penelope to the point of delirium. She, following her father's vocation, was training to sell books and worked as a clerk in the main shopping area, the agora between the harbor docks and the Street of the Soma. Starting at six o'clock in the morning, when the sun was already high, she worked till five in the afternoon and then was free to meet me. We loved walking and sightseeing in the Gamma district, where were located the administration buildings and the royal palace—the former royal residence—as well as the museum, which contained more objects of art than those of Rome and Athens and was an advanced study center as well, all of which were adjacent to the port for the imperial flotilla.

From the Gamma district were the connections to canals linking Alexandria to the Nile. Also within this district, which took up a quarter of all the city space, were the temples to the various gods. Adjacent to the nearby Great Library were several splendid parks where grew many exotic plants. To me these were all familiar, to Penelope mainly new, and I loved seeing her reactions with fresh eyes.

The shop in the area where Penelope worked sold everything from fruits and vegetables to the most exquisite gold jewelry. Alexandrian glassware was known throughout the empire, as well as the woven textiles. Most distinctive and of value were the pages made in Alexandria from the native papyrus, used in the finest books.

I bought Penelope gold earrings and a thick gold ring inscribed "Forever" in florid Greek letters: the fact that I was rich and she poor must have been a factor but not one I thought of. My love—perhaps better defined as a mixture of worshipful feeling and intense lust—was overwhelming, and the scent of her body from the hot sun, the touch of her golden-tinted skin, the jiggle of her breasts and thighs as she walked—not to mention the kisses we began to exchange—were driving me mad. Philosophy be damned, religion be damned, I wanted her as a man lusts for the flesh of the woman he loves no matter what.

But it was impossible, or seemed impossible, for us to find a place to make love. I could not of course take her to our mansion, staffed at all times with servants, nor she to her father's house. We dared not rent a room in the brothel area for fear of scandal. The beautiful parks were filled with people at all hours and the bathhouses separated men from women.

At first I thought I had found a solution. It was to visit the Pharos, the world's tallest lighthouse, built of white stone on the isolated island of the same name, so high—a walk up of 135 meters—that nobody, I thought, would ascend to the top. There we could be free to indulge my passion. That she would consent I had small doubt since by hints she'd told me that I was not the first man she would know as a woman. This was not surprising, for most adolescents in Alexandria started young under that hot sun.

The island of Pharos was linked to the mainland by a mole, the Heptastadium, which was seven meters wide and separated the sea into two parts, the large Megar Limen, or Great Port, and the smaller Eunostos, or Port of Good Hope, both swarming with fishing and pleasure boats. The Roman fleet also used the Megar Limen as its anchorage. The walk itself to the lighthouse was thrilling because the rich of Alexandria owned large yachts and gave continuous parties which we could overlook while walking to the island.

But I was wrong. To begin with, Alexandria was one of the most famous sightseeing cities of the world and it seemed that everyone wanted to visit the celebrated lighthouse. It was entered by a long ramp which circled the building, leading to an observation deck. I found to my annoyance that paid guides worked there. The second level, reached by a winding staircase with continuous windows, had even more breathtaking views, but also guides soliciting money. The third level was open at the top with a large curved mirror to enlarge the flames lighting the waterways at night. Topping the roof was an enormous statue of the god Zeus Soter. It was a fabulous trip for a tourist, of whom there were many, but not for a young man seething with passion to make love to his girlfriend. I was so disgusted I glared at Zeus and he seemed in my imagination to bend forward and glare back at me.

Returning to the city on the Heptastadium, we leaned over the protective railing to watch the pleasure boats buoyed alongside. Several parties were in progress and we heard the music and the laughing.

"Will you take me on a trip in one of those beautiful boats?" Penelope asked.

"How can I? I have no money."

"But my father says your family is one of the richest in all Egypt."

"Somewhat exaggerated," I said defensively. "Besides, what is my father's is his and not mine. He did say, however, that if my grades at the academy were in the top one percent when I graduate in a few months, he'd treat me to a trip."

"Where?" Penelope asked.

"I don't know. He just said a trip." Excited at the thought of traveling with Penelope, I put my arm around her shoulders. She turned and smiled with those emerald eyes that ignited my universe.

Then it happened. That was many decades ago and the experience was not repeated but it will never leave me. I was looking over the railing. The sky was blue with a few floating clouds. The water was blue, without a ripple. The far shore was wrapped in a blue haze that seemed an endless extent of the sea. The pleasure boats had white sails, some furled, some unfurled. The sails on those unfurled flapped as if alive. White and grey gulls glided above in the blue.

I repeat, then it happened. Perhaps it was because of Penelope's emerald eyes, which seemed to unscroll eternity. But suddenly I was without body, wrapped in a silent motionless serenity, without time or space, but so peaceful and profound that in that instant I understood what some of the truly religious people had written about, something the cynic and skeptic Greek philosophers I had studied either missed or ignored. It was an endless bliss, a serene nonbeing in an eternity of warmth and sunlight, what some call spirit or soul or love, beyond and above the petty self. And at last I understood what my Uncle Philo wrote about.

It lasted seconds. I came back to reality with a jolt because Penelope was shaking me. "Do you feel all right?" she asked. "For a moment it seemed like you were far away."

I thought of trying to explain but it seemed impossible to describe what I felt. Lamely I said, "It is your beautiful emerald eyes. They make me drunk with love." But the truth was that though Penelope may have been the motive, the sense of beatific eternity was not of her doing; better put, she may have been the springboard for what I felt, but not the feeling itself.

I repeat that it never happened again despite my many triumphs and, at the end, my years of sickness and introspection. As I dictate these words to Isocrates, my educated Greek slave, I think to feel what I felt, the beatitude of the soul or spirit, one needs a stimulus of some sort, a kind of religious ecstasy, perhaps a cradle of love, to kindle such an ascent of being. And from that moment on, through the many sordid episodes of my rise to the top of the Roman world, I never again would mock those who strove, like my Uncle Philo, to reach what they conceived as Yahweh. So I suppose at bottom I was really a shallow Epicurean; or else my early religious background had grasped me underground and come at last to the surface in my sickness and old age to haunt me and my conscience.

VIII

But my sharp body need for Penelope would not leave; I might love the spirit but I also craved the flesh. And at last I found a solution, a crazy solution, but a solution.

Outside the walls to the west of the city of Alexandria laid a vast cemetery, "the city of the dead," or Necropolis as it was called, as immense in its graves of the dead as the homes of the living within the city. The social classes had different graves. The poorest were buried directly in the ground in coarse white sheets. Persons of the middle class were buried in body-sized niches or recesses hollowed out of the soft Alexandrian rock, almost like large honeycombs. The rich had whole suites, with oil lamps, incense burners, painted walls, and different rooms; beds in the bedrooms, and dining rooms with chairs and tables where on certain holy days the living family would gather to eat their meats in common with their dead ancestors.

As a boy, fascinated by this Necropolis, I with my brother and several fearless comrades used to explore the huge cemetery, and I knew not only the holy days when the families met but which of the underground graves were the most luxurious. And we would have no problem going through the city wall gates to the Necropolis because, with no longer any external threat, they were left open by the guards.

The shocking but delicious thought that came to me was here was where Penelope and I would never be disturbed. When I proposed this to her she was astounded and said no immediately. But after I brought it up a few times she agreed "to take a look."

It was dark but cool underground. I lit a multi-wick oil lamp and remembered a "bedroom," a room with beds and a sofa. I guided Penelope to the room. The flickering wicks with grotesque shadows thrown on the white plastered walls frightened Penelope and she clung to me. I sat with her on the bed, stretched out and, in violent lust, I simply took her physically—the long pent-up desire was so great I suppose I acted in a brutal way.

Penelope screamed. Her scream ricocheted against the walls of the room and came back in receding echoes. "You are horrible," she said and cried. I, gazing into her tear-filled emerald eyes, still excited, never left her body but stayed inside. Plunging again, my body tight against hers, the feel of her breasts against my chest, I came again. This time I felt her insides throbbing. She had stopped crying and began to move her body in rhythm with my short plunges. I could sense she was responding. I was slower but still hard and she panted, "Yes, oh yes," and then amusingly, "you are horrible, darling," as I came again. I ran my hands through her flaxen hair, caressing her ears and lowering my head, sucked her breasts. I got excited and entered her again, this time with no objection. My lust satisfied, kissing her lips, I got up and said, "You are the most wonderful thing Zeus ever created, if there is a Zeus. I adore you. I will adore you forever."

Then I got a shock. She stood up from the bed, smoothed her dress, and said: "When are we getting married?" It was like I was hit by a rock. Marriage for me, still an adolescent just finishing the academy, with no determined future, was as remote an idea as my jumping off a shoulder of Zeus Soter standing atop the Pharos lighthouse. Love to me was an ideality, a beautiful gift of nature of which Penelope was the purest symbol; marriage was a social duty for money, position, and power, unrelated to love. Love was beauty; marriage was duty. There was no relation between the two.

"Married?" I stuttered.

"Why not?" Penelope asked. "People our age marry all the time."

I put my head down. I could think of no reply.

"Now that you've had me, things look different," she said with remorseless logic. "I am Greek, poor, uneducated, and with no background. You are a Jew, rich, educated, and with a background that may take you far."

I still said nothing because I could think of nothing to say. I tried to kiss her but she pushed me away. "I hope I get pregnant," Penelope said sharply.

I shivered. The thought had never come to me. I rearranged my pants. "We had better go," I said. "It's getting late."

Without a word Penelope went to the exit of the underground apartment and, not waiting for me, started up the steps to the Necropolis surface. I rushed to follow her. She said nothing as we walked back together.

"Penelope, I swear to you by everything sacred that I love you. I want to continue our relation. You are the only woman I've ever loved and probably the only woman I ever will."

"Then prove it by marrying me," she said seriously.

"I can't. I *cannot.* You don't understand."

"I understand only too well," she said coldly.

"But life isn't that simple," I said. "We live in a network of duties, of responsibilities, of family obligations. I can't at this point of my life just get up and marry."

"I've told you the reasons before so I won't repeat them," she said. Then her voice softened. "I believe you when you say you love me. And believe it or not I love you too—your intelligence, your drive, your willpower. You will go far in this world. But you don't want to take me with you."

I tried to kiss her. Even after making love several times her look thrilled me. But she pushed me away. "Go back to your mansion," she said. "I'll go back to our small house." Then she added something which shocked me. "At least," she said, "we are Macedonians, not descendants of Asiatic Bedouins."

I passed the next days in utter misery. I couldn't eat and was afraid to drink wine for I might babble something. My mother was frightened and wanted to call a doctor but I refused. Every late afternoon I went to the base of the steps of the Great Library, waiting for hours, but Penelope never appeared. I even considered suicide in the way lovesick adolescents do but didn't have the courage.

At last I thought of a way which might work, appealing to her sense of humor, which was great. At the academy we had studied the top Latin poets and I went to my textbook of Latin poetry to see if I could find a poem that might appeal to her and possibly soften her feelings toward me. The one I picked was by the famous poet Ovid, banished from Rome due to his erotic poetry. I wrote out a copy and slipped it under the door to Penelope's house, folded in a fine papyrus on which were written the words, "To Penelope, my Helena, lovely daughter of Zeus."

AFTERNOON DIVERSIONS

It was a summer afternoon: the lattice by my bed,
One shutter closed, about the room a pleasant darkness shed,
Such as in a forest oft you see, or when the twilight fades,
Or in the dusk of early dawn, well suited to fair maids
Who love to hide beneath its cloak their looks of modest shame:
And when it was, in tunic clad, Corinna to me came,
Her hair unbound about her neck, presage of future bliss,
More beautiful than Lais or than queen Semiramis.

At once I drew her tunic down—the fabric was so fine
That what it hid a lover's eye could easily divine—
She tried, 'tis true, to stay me; but t'was very plain to see
That in our amorous strife she did not wish for victory,
And self-betrayed at last she stood, the tunic flung aside,
In all the flawless splendor of her beauty's naked pride.

I saw her shoulders and her arms and marked their loveliness;
I touched the apples of her breasts made for fond caress;
I gazed upon her bosom and the smooth white plain below,
Her rounded flanks and slender thighs with youthful strength aglow.

But why say more, when every part alike was passing fair?
Unveiled I took her in my arms and held her captive there.
You know the rest. Worn out with love wearied at length we lay.
Such afternoons as this I hope may often come my way.

No reply. I waited again at the steps of the Great Library. She never appeared. After about ten days I did receive an answer but it was not from Penelope. It was from her father and written in stiff formal Greek as one might expect from a librarian.

Dear Mr. Tiberius Julius Alexander:

Let me begin by congratulating you on the name of Alexander, though how you and your family got it is of mystery to me—to us, rather, my daughter Penelope and me.

Your conduct toward my daughter fell far short of that extraordinary Greek, Alexander of Macedon, from whom I am proud to say, unlike certain Alexandrians regardless of name, I inherit his bloodline. That said, enough.

Penelope has told me of your ungentlemanly conduct—to say the least—and has no desire to continue any type of conduct with you. I hope you comprehend what I mean because, though a mere librarian to you, I too have a sense when it is appropriate to leave certain things unsaid. I trust you understand me. As we say in Greek, my daughter feels toward you what is conveyed by the word *bdelygma*, though the literal translation of "loathing" might be too mild.

Enough. As an admirer of your Uncle Philo I wish you do not suffer from the wrath of Zeus for an ignoble act.

Sarapion, son of Sosipatros Timoclea

It was finished. I now knew it. I would never see Penelope again though I wondered just what she had told her father since it had been so easy to enter her body. I was sure, remembering certain of her discreet innuendos, that what I had done was not the first time.

IX

It seemed that my life in late adolescence bumped into one crisis after another. It must have been several months later when there came another great change for me, this one at the same time as my graduation from the Arista academy. It was a serious riot by the Alexandrian Greeks, envious that the Jews, about one-third of the city's population, controlled most of the money. The mobs invaded our quarter and only by a miracle did our mansion escape sacking.

It was then that my father called a family conclave, my father and mother, Uncle Philo, Marcus and me. He shut the door to the library so the servants couldn't hear.

"I'm frightened," my father said. "The tension between we Jews and the Greeks is growing more and more serious. With the 5th and 10th Roman legions practicing in the Thebaid for a possible Ethiopian campaign, we are not protected from serious mob action. Besides, who knows what the legions would do? I don't have to tell you that Lucius Aelius Sejanus, the favorite of Emperor Tiberius, hates us and exiled the Roman Jews to work in the mines of Sardegna, a most unhealthy place.

"As for you, Philo, I am less concerned. Besides your many Greek friends, the chief librarian of our Great Library would always give you shelter. As for myself and my wife I have made secure arrangements. It is for you, Tiberius and Marcus, that I am most concerned."

My father smiled at Marcus. "Did I ever tell you that you were named after Marcus Antonius, 'Auntie' Antonia's father? Her mother of course was Octavius Caesar's daughter, now Divus Augustus, for which reason he did not kill Antonia as he did Cleopatra's brother and her son by Julius Caesar. Fate has smiled on us since 'Auntie' Antonia [my father called her 'Auntie' though of course Antonia was not his aunt] has left all her Egyptian property in my care and I am most scrupulous in its supervision.

"Marcus, getting back to the point," my father continued, "you know we have our main warehouses at Canopus, a very short distance from Alexandria. Any organized mob could sack them.

"What I am going to do, Marcus, is to build new warehouses at Koptos, where we now have our goods coming across the Nile in the south. No Greek mob would go that far into the Thebaid. You will supervise the construction and can live nearby at Thebes, which though provincial and hot is not a bad town; they even have Greek-style gymnasiums and a theatre, though mostly attended by Nubians. And in one of the towns a short distance away there is a small *proseuche*, which I attend when at Koptos on business."

I saw Marcus start to protest. He was still a rather young adolescent, and at his age who would want to be buried at Koptos for many months? My father anticipated this.

"Marcus, I swear to you it won't be a long time. You should have no fear because our Nubian guards are very faithful—they hate the Greeks more than we do—and besides, the 5th legion is spread along the Nile towns and would prevent any disorder. Even though Commander Lucius Trisasea Sabinus has just retired to his beloved Pompeii, I have made similar arrangements with his successor."

Marcus, an obedient child, flushed but said nothing. He gave a side-glance at our mother but she shrugged her shoulders hopelessly.

"As for you, Tiberius," my father continued, "the Roman lover of the family, I have made arrangements that will please you and might knock some sense in your head about the Romans, their vicious attitude toward their slaves, their disregard for human life and dignity, even including the highest nobility who now cringe before Emperor Tiberius despite his disgusting depravity."

"To Rome!" I said excitedly.

"Yes, to Rome for about six months. I have a business matter you can handle for me there. It doesn't take a legal education, just common sense. And that I know you have. In the meantime we rich Jews are pulling strings in Rome to see that our praefectus takes a stronger position about these riots. 'Auntie' Antonia has arranged that you will stay with the son of an old friend of hers. It would be unseemly that an elderly woman have a young man living in her house."

"You have all the luck," Marcus said to me bitterly. "Why couldn't I have been the older son?"

Our father ignored the remark. "Both of you get ready to travel. Marcus, it's already arranged that you will go down to Koptos on our next caravan. Tiberius, passage has been booked on a boat, the *Olympus*. You leave in three days."

I went to my father and kissed him, possibly the first or second time in my life. He looked embarrassed. My mother just sat there with tears running down her cheeks. She was right, though we did not know it, for this was the end of our family life together.

Of course I now realize that my trip to Rome was planned for another reason. One of my father's Roman associates could have handled the matter, but my father must have gotten wind of my affair. After all, for months Penelope and I had walked along the two main boulevards of Alexandria hand in hand, often kissing, and without doubt it was reported that I was having a liaison, not only a liaison but one with a Greek girl of unknown background. Like rich fathers from time immemorial facing this problem, the easiest solution was to send the errant son on a trip, any trip long enough to kill the danger of an improper union. Sending me thus to Rome was a convenient subterfuge.

X

The following letters, written by Tiberius Julius Alexander to his father, brother, and Uncle Philo, are transcripts of actual letters sent and then conveyed much later by Isocrates, his educated Greek slave, to the Great Library in Alexandria.

My dear Father,

Salve. Everything fine?

You asked me to give an account of my life in Rome. I haven't written for two weeks because I waited to have more precise impressions.

"Auntie" Antonia is an old, sick, but delightful lady with marvelous stories about events in the reign of Divus Augustus and, told with acidity, those of Emperor Tiberius. The most amazing tale to me, coming from our background, was how Livia, the strong-willed wife of Divus Augustus, by agreement with her husband arranged to provide sixteen-year-old Syrian girls—his sexual preference—for his bed. I do admit, however, there are limits and I find the accounts of Tiberius with his *spintriae*, his boy whores, just disgusting. "Auntie" Antonia seems unafraid to tell these stories but I notice before talking she peers around to be sure no slaves are listening. Apparently as Emperor Tiberius has grown older he has not only become more sexually depraved but crueler as well. In fact, Antonia quoted the most recent witty verse making the rounds among the aristocracy.

Fastidit vinum quia iam sitit iste curorem
Tam bibit hunc avide, quam bibit ante merum.

Since I am not sure of your literary Latin, that means:

Wine does he loathe, because now of blood he has a thirst.
He drinks that as greedily as wine he did at first.

Nice thing to write about our emperor! In fact his nickname with the top nobility is *Caprinicus*, or "Goat-like," a takeoff that like a Capra or goat he has isolated himself on the island of Capri.

As you arranged through "Auntie" Antonia, I am staying with a charming young man about my age, Antonio Julius Lepidus, a Julio-Claudian, who believes that with my name I belong by gens to the same line as he does rather than through adoption; and that I am a pure Roman from Egypt rather than an Egyptian, and certainly not a Jew, for like most Romans he loathes "inferior" peoples. Though my pride is offended, I hold my tongue. If "Auntie" Antonia said nothing, why should I?

Antonio Julius Lepidus is an admirable host. He is slated to be a centurion next winter but until then, lacking intellectual interests, has little to do but spend the rest of his family fortune in dicing or going to the Circus, where he is a passionate backer of the Green team of charioteers. He is great fun though not too bright, a passionate Roman patriot, fearless and a true believer in the imperial system. He will make an excellent officer and probably rise high in the military ranks.

Now to business. Following instructions, I called Gnaeus Ponteius Capito, one of your business partners here in Rome. His freedman, obviously expecting me, gave instructions how to drive to his villa.

I don't recall you telling me whether you've visited him here but in case not I want you to know he lives in magnificent style somewhat outside the city limits. I took a *brota*, a two-wheeled carriage, through the Porta Capena, the city gate leading to the Appian Way. Along the highway are huge tombs of the ancient Roman families until you get farther out.

Gnaeus Ponteius Capito lives on a side road ascending a hill. The entrance is blocked by a tall iron-slatted gateway. When I pulled up to the gate my two horses stopped short, neighed and pawed the ground. Then I heard what frightened them. It was the low but ominous growling of dogs.

I got out and went to the gate. Peering through the slats, I could see two huge mastiffs rearing but held in check on chains by a guard. I then saw the sign *CAVE CANEM*, or Beware of the Dog.

"Tiberius Julius Alexander," I called out.

The guard, having received notice of my coming, spoke to the dogs. They instantly quieted. He pulled them to one side, unlatched the gate from the inside, pushed it open, and motioned for me to come in.

I lashed my horses forward and up a dirt road, shaded on both sides by cypress trees, and to the villa. It had a wonderful view of the land below.

I was met at the door by your business partner. You of course must know him but I will tell you as I saw him. About your age, stocky, he had the usual Roman face, fair skin, a long slightly hooked nose, and a full head of dark hair hanging over his forehead and cut below his ears. Though he was smiling, his pursed thin lips gave an overall somber and forceful expression.

"Welcome, Tiberius Julius Alexander, son of Gaius Julius," he said, as usual emphasizing the "Julius," the highest-class Roman name. "Twice welcome. Before we get to business, which will take no time, let me give you a brief tour of my villa and grounds. First, would you like a glass of good wine?"

"No thanks," I said. I wanted to keep my wits and one glass almost always led to another.

"Come into the atrium," my host said. This was the inner open courtyard around which the rooms were built. It was supported by spaced marble columns set on the marble floor. Even the walls were marble, with statues spaced alongside. I noticed there were no windows, probably because of security concerns. Large braziers held a liquid, I presumed olive oil, to heat the rooms at night or in the cold Roman winters. Also for light at night were broad earthenware holders with many-wicked candles.

"Would you like to see a typical room?" he asked. "I've never been to Egypt in my earlier army career as a centurion, but I'd be curious as to how your father's mansion differs from mine." He led me to what was a dining room. The chairs and tables were of rare wood inlaid with ivory. Couches were for men, chairs being for the women and the old. The sideboards were loaded with gold and silver spoons, as well as cups and dishes.

I was impressed but determined not to show it. "Pretty much the same as with us," I said. "We decorate more; it is an ancient Egyptian tradition."

He smiled, a bit ironically, but said nothing. "Let me take you to the gardens," he said.

This was truly another world and one only twenty miles from the center of Rome! His "gardens" were really a small park. Aside from the many cypresses, as well as other tree types which I didn't know because they were not native to Egypt, there were long arbors with grape vines, a large field planted with fruit and vegetables, even a circular fishpond, all of which, my host said, supplied the food and even some of the wine for the villa. Scattered throughout were marble and bronze statues. I couldn't believe my eyes; I even saw a peacock strut by.

"By Jupiter, this is something," I managed to stammer.

"Now you see why your father doesn't have to worry about my overdue payment on his last shipment of pearls and emeralds," Gnaeus Ponteius Capito said.

"There was never such a question," I said diplomatically.

We went back to the villa. This time I accepted one glass of wine. "Your father, Gaius Julius, wrote me you were more interested in an administrative or military career than going into private business in Egypt," my host said. "Is that true?"

"Military," I said.

"A wise decision," he said. "Business can be up and down. I've been very fortunate but one never knows. *Dis aliter visum*; as Virgil wrote in the *Aeneid*, 'We may propose but the gods dispose.' In business that's the way it is. In military, especially as a Julio-Claudian, you'll have a secure career. And after your service, still relatively young and with a good pension, you can then go into business." He laughed. "Presuming you don't get killed."

Gnaeus Ponteius Capito walked me to the main villa door. "Your father is lucky," he said. "He has you and, I understand, a younger brother. My villa may be beautiful but I have no sons. My line ends with me. Write that to your father. Tell him I support your thought of first entering the army, as a centurion of course."

And I am so doing.

Our Yahweh be with you
Your son, Tiberius

My dear Brother Marcus,

I suppose father told you that I'm staying with a young man about my age, Antonio Julius Lepidus. (He is by blood and not adoption of the Julio-Claudian line.) This is through wonderful "Auntie" Antonia.

At first I thought Antonio, though charming, was not too bright and was also a bit boring. But I've discovered another side of his character which impresses me greatly. It's his incredible patriotism despite the obvious immoral antics of the emperor. I will give you one example. The mausoleum of Divus Augustus includes not only his ashes but those of the immediate members of his family. Formerly it was open to any Roman citizen but several years ago someone attempted to steal the golden urn in which rest the emperor's ashes. Now only persons of noble birth are admitted, naturally including my host, Antonio Julius Lepidus. As he was known to the guards, after vouching for me as a Julio-Claudian family member as well, we were admitted into the dark chamber with only a high-set clerestory placed so that the sunlight played on the urn of the great emperor, which shimmered in golden haze. The clerestory was set in such a way that no matter what the daylight hour the urn of Divus Augustus glittered. A series of other gold urns holding the ashes of close family members were set alongside. Across the shallow corridor were cedar wood benches. My friend sat down on one and I sat alongside. Antonio, almost always playful and jesting, said not a word. After what seemed many minutes, he spoke.

"Tiberius?"

"Yes?"

"Do you feel what I feel? There are enclosed the sacred ashes of Divus Augustus alongside those of his uncle, Julius Caesar, the two greatest Romans who ever lived. Do you sense their presence?"

"Yes," I said, though I did not.

"I pray to their spirit and feel Jupiter hears my plea."

"What plea?"

"That someday I may act, in no matter how small a way, to live up to the glory of being a Julio-Claudian, to justify Jupiter's gift to me for my ancestry, perhaps to die for Rome, even to exalt in the thought of dying for our glorious Rome. *Dulce et decorum est pro patria mori.* That is my most fervent wish. And something in me says that Jupiter hears and will answer my prayer. Could you pledge me something, Tiberius?"

"What?"

"Who knows the future? We both want to enter the military. Could you pledge, if possible, that if you are near when I die you will arrange that my ashes be buried in this sacred mausoleum?"

"Antonio, don't talk that way," I said.

"Promise. I have no brothers or sisters and I consider you a very close friend even though we've known each other a short time."

"I promise," I said, with tears coming to my eyes.

He kissed my cheek. "And I will do the same for you," he said. "I swear it."

Antonio lapsed into silence. Then abruptly he got up, went to the entry door, kneeled toward the gold urns, and left. He hardly said another word the rest of the day.

Marcus, that is why I say Rome will last for centuries, if not forever, if the city can produce men like Antonio Julius Lepidus.

I had another very interesting experience with Antonio. It came through "Auntie" Antonia, who is now a very important person since the deaths of the sons of Divus Augustus, in what I may add seem suspicious circumstances. Now her son Claudius—though considered a halfwit—is one of the few potential aspirants to become emperor since Tiberius is so old. Antonia, knowing that the two of us are interested in a military career, arranged through her influence that we visit a training camp for legionnaires near Rome. We both jumped at the chance.

A centurion met us at the gated entrance after we crossed the moat. The centurion then guided us to the praetorium, the military headquarters. There he knocked at the door. "Centurion Publius Crassus," he said stiffly.

"By Jupiter, I'm busy. Come back later," a voice bellowed.

"Centurion Publius Crassus, with two guests who claim they've been sent to see the camp. Antonio Julius Lepidus and Tiberius Julius," the legionnaire stated, winking at Antonio. I noticed that my name Alexander, a non-Roman name, was not mentioned. My friend Antonio had thought it wiser not to mention the Greek name of Alexander.

There was a muffled oath, a loud click as though a closet door was closed, and then an interval which I thought was probably devoted to arranging his clothes and pulling up his boots. Antonio smiled at me. We both had the same thought. The commander was "entertaining" a guest, though being in Rome we did not know male or female.

"Welcome." The door to the office opened. In it appeared a ruddy-faced middle-aged man, stocky, with hands like heavy mitts. "The most honorable Antonia Nero Drusus informed through a courier that two aristocratic gentlemen would visit me." He hastily buttoned his military jacket.

"I understand you two most esteemed gentlemen are interested in an army career. Good! We need noble patriotic Romans; the army is being flooded with freedmen and farmers, good enough to fight, I grant you, but not to lead. Too many aristocrats have become lazy and effeminate."

I admired his honesty. It was true, though I reflected that as long as there were young aristocrats like my friend Antonio, Rome would still be secure.

"What would you like to see? Commander Quintus Piso at your service." He reached over and pulled more tightly his high boots. I noticed he glanced at his garment closet and then spoke in a louder voice, "We can leave immediately."

"We'd like to see the legionnaire training grounds," Antonio said. I let him do the talking; my Egyptian accent was still strong.

"Follow me." He opened the front door and after we passed through, closed it with a loud bang. "Beautiful day, gentlemen," he said and led us down a path to a central area so large it could well have been a park. "Here is where recruits train," Commander Piso said. "They are all volunteers. We have no compulsory enlistment except in emergencies, like the Punic Wars. What a military genius that Hannibal was," he said. "After he utterly destroyed our armies at Cannae, if instead of waiting he had marched north immediately, Rome was helpless. A military genius . . . and a fool," he added. "We never make such mistakes. Smash the enemy. Smash them again, and sell the men and women as slaves. That's the way war should be made; that's why we are masters of the world. Carthage and Corinth were left smoking ruins. That's how I think wars must be fought. *Lex talionis*—root them out."

The open space within what seemed a small amphitheatre was filled with men in different groups. "The first thing they learn," the commander said, pointing to one group, "is marching in rank and running in order, as well as swimming in warmer weather. Then, over there," he said, pointing, "is weapon training, at first with round wickerwork shields and wooden staves, both of double weight. A tall heavy stake is planted deep into the ground and the recruits aim at all points, striking against the top, the middle, the base of the stake as though it were a living enemy. Then the recruit is given real weapons—notice to the left side—and repeats the same action. The final stage," he said, "is there," pointing, "where each recruit is matched against another in actual combat. Failing to measure up"—

and Commander Piso nodded toward the seats in what seemed the amphitheatre where centurions were watching to judge the performance—"they are either dismissed or given their rations in barley instead of wheat, and not restored until a centurion is satisfied with their performance. The training swords, however, are tipped with a leather button to prevent serious injury. They are then set in mock fights matched in pairs.

"That is not the end. After mastering attacks with the sword comes the same training with a spear, hurled at some distance at those stakes, this time, however, equipped with bronze shields, breastplates, helmets, and leg armor.

"If all this is approved by the centurions watching, they are admitted as legionnaires, though they still have to carry three days' rations in forced marches of some forty kilometers with full equipment as the last step. *Usus promptos facit*; they are now ready."

"By Jupiter," Antonio said, "I am losing a bit of enthusiasm. I frankly don't think I could stand up under that training."

Commander Quintus Piso laughed. "You wouldn't go through that training as a Julio-Claudian. You would start off as a centurion and learn in that position whatever was necessary. Do you think that Divus Augustus or Emperor Tiberius was a legionnaire?! They *commanded* them from above. The top army ranks are held by stalwart men like you from our best class. With skill and some luck you might even become a commander. Do you think I, a Piso, went through that training?" He laughed heartily.

As we were leaving, Antonio pointed to a curious formation of trainees. There were three lines of soldiers, standing rigidly behind each other. The front line held swords and shields, slashing at an invisible foe. At a signal they broke off action and dropped back, while the second line rushed forward to take their place. The process was then repeated with the third line.

"What is that?" Antonio asked. "It looks like a game."

"Some game!" snorted the commander. "That is our famous *triplex acies*, the triple battle line which has won us many battles. Usually a Roman soldier fights at close range for fifteen minutes before the second and then the third line replace him. The enemy, no matter how brave, is thus met every quarter-hour by a fresh

Roman soldier. Against such a tactic the fatigued enemy soldiers finally despair and break ranks."

"How clever," Antonio said.

"And that's why we are masters of the world, having developed such tactics. And you too," Commander Piso added, "may in turn contribute to enlarging still more our great empire." He stamped a boot for emphasis.

Needless to say, Marcus, this all whetted my appetite. I don't want to spend my life with books of accounting, my brother, which you don't seem to mind. I want to see Graecia, Syria, Mauretania, Armenia, Britannia, Parthia, Germania, whatever! You can make the money stuck at Koptos. I want adventure.

One last related note, though this of course is strictly between us. They have the most beautiful whores in the world. In fact they come from all over and are in every color, size, and shape—not too expensive either since there are so many. My taste is for the girls from Germania with blond hair and blue eyes. Sometimes even green. I didn't tell you but I had a serious relation at home, and never stop thinking of her except in the arms of these pliant bodies, where I try to imagine it's her.

P.S. I heard an interesting rumor from "Auntie." She told me our father wrote that you are showing interest in Princess Berenice, daughter of King Agrippa of Judaea. How can that be? Isn't she only eleven or twelve? I've heard, however, she is very beautiful.

Your brother, Tiberius

My dear Uncle Philo,

I am well and hope you are too. Life has been fascinating for me in this great metropolis, the greatest in the world, and I am comfortably lodged thanks to father's great friend, "Auntie" Antonia. Indeed, through her aid I am staying with a young man of the highest aristocracy who treats me as an equal due to our both being of the Julio-Claudian line (he doesn't know it is mine by adoption and not by blood). His name is Antonio Julius Lepidus and he is preparing for a military career. As I've learned, aristocrats opting for the military start off as centurions, that is, over a hundred legionnaires, and Antonio took me to one center where I was fascinated to watch the training to be a legionnaire.

But enough of the military. I know you are more interested in religious beliefs and rites of the Roman people, and for your sake I have made many queries and visited their temples. It is also of great interest to me because their religious ways here are almost the contrary of ours.

I don't have to review the names of the Roman gods and goddesses (though their precise functions are still largely a mystery to me) because you, I am certain, know more of them than I ever could. There are temples and priests provided by the state but the average Roman citizen has little to do with any official rites. Citizens do use them, let me make that clear, but it is only to pray for a special favor such as a cure from a disease or help in love. They pay a fee for such requests and the priests, so they say, are quite rich as a result. I may add that the temples themselves are rather simple in design, often small structures, usually a long room housing a statue of a god or goddess. Very often I have been told the statues were stolen from Graecia.

Curiously, there are no organized services such as ours, and prayers and chants are performed solely by the priests. I tried to learn more about these priestly services but no one seemed to know what they were. How different from us!

Distinct from the priests are an order called the *augurs*. There are sixteen and their duty is to tell whether the gods like or dislike a proposed action of the state. These signs come from the flight of birds, from thunder, or from the way chickens eat their food! They sincerely believe in what they call *malis avibus*, "bad birds," whereupon they will avoid an action. The opposite, approving an action, are *avibus bonis*. Also there are *haruspices*, soothsayers who examine the vital organs, such as the liver of animals sacrificed by the priests, a custom I was told was taken over from the Etruscans.

How strange! To think these Romans, with such odd religious customs, are the people who've conquered almost the whole world. Maybe one reason is their indifference to organized state religion! The proof is that when Divus Augustus took over Rome he found scarcely a hundred temples in the enormous population and had to repair from disuse many of them.

Actually, from what I can gather, the real religion of the Romans is not temple worship or any organized religious communal centers—the very opposite of us—but rather the *lares familiaris*, household deities, little statuettes which are the guardians of their homes. Likewise are the *penates*. In general it might be said that the *lares* relate to ancestor worship while the *penates* keep the house from danger. Before these deities daily acts of reverence take place, simple requests such as asking for their protection. Those who are too poor to own them worship at *lares publici*, which are these figures placed at popular crossroads. I may add an amusing fact. When a Roman swears to the gods, he clutches his testicles! I was told that comes from the word *testari*, to call to.

You may also be interested to know that other religions, or rather superstitions, are starting to make headway in Rome. Astrology, frowned upon and attacked by their great statesman Cicero, is growing among the former farmers who've lost their land and cling to any hope. Yet even stranger than astrology are the mystery cults from the East. An important cult imported from our Egypt is that of the Mother Goddess Isis, whose image is a young cow. With her is associated Serapis, a chief god among the deities of our country—you of course know that cult. There is a temple devoted to the two deities in the Campus Martius, the old military training fields.

Actually, as foreign cults go, the strongest—especially among the soldiers—is Mithraism, the cult of Celestial Light, which has come here from Parthia and India. Its strongest appeal is the doctrine of the immortal soul (somewhat as our Jewish Pharisees think) and that those who believe will go after death to eternal life. Mithraism has a particular appeal among the poor, for its "truth" is relevant equally for slaves and manual laborers as well as the upper classes. It thus in a sense champions the downtrodden. Its weakness to me is both because it does not allow women to join and it also has very elaborate initiation rites. In that sense our religion (and even the perverted Yeshua sect) has more appeal.

I believe such cults, by their ritual and antiquity, touch the emotion of the common people more than rather impersonal Roman religion. Which reminds me. Remember that silly meeting we attended in Alexandria run by a man named Mark, who claimed to be a Jew but worshiped a certain Yeshua, Jesus in Latin? Believe it or not, I ran into a woman at a party—and an aristocrat no less—who claimed she too believed in that Jewish sect and that a small group of them meet every week to pray together!

I will be back in Alexandria soon and have taken more notes of the religious customs here which may be of interest to you. I must end this letter frankly to state that I am now more convinced than ever that all the religious "mysteries," and I include our own, seem a bit bogus to me. They can't all be right; they might indeed all be wrong and the ancient Greek skeptics may be closer to the truth—whatever that is. One thing of which I am convinced, and now more than ever, is of Roman might and the Roman military system that buttresses it.

Nunc scripsi totum, da mihi potem: having written so much, give me a drink! And thus I am bringing back for you a bottle of the best Falerian wine for us to drink together.

Your nephew,
Tiberius

Dear Marcus,

I wrote only a few days ago, and I'll be home shortly, but I can't resist writing again to tell you what to me was an extraordinary experience.

You may recall we once went to the Hippodrome in Alexandria. I seem to remember you were only twelve but you begged me to take you along. I bet my week's allowance on a charioteer by the name of Hakim—I simply liked the name—but he overturned, losing my money, and I threatened to beat you if you told father. Remember?

Well, my friend Antonio Julius Lepidus suggested we go to the Circus Maximus here, which he hadn't done with me before because he's a heavy gambler and was short of money. But last week he won a neat pile at dicing, so we went.

Our Hippodrome, the equivalent of their Circus, is like a mouse compared to a rhino. The one here is simply enormous, some half mile long and a quarter that in width. On the long sides and one of the shorter ones runs a canal over three meters wide and deep to stop wild animals from entering the stands when the Circus is sometimes used for animal fights. Three rows of seats rise along these sides, the first row in stone, the second and third rows in wood. The other short side contains the starting boxes for the chariots, which are frail platforms usually drawn by two or four horses. A rope opens the boxes at the same time. The short side is also the main entrance.

Antonio told me that the seats hold over 100,000 persons and, believe me Marcus, the crowd was enormous, enormous! Only aristocrats or plebeians of influence can sit on the lowest row of stone seats and a praetorian checks those coming in. The guard recognized Antonio and he in turn vouched for me as a Julio-Claudian.

We were between races when we sat down and Antonio

regaled me with stories. He said the Circus was the only public place of entertainment in Rome which allowed women to sit together with men and it was a great pick-up spot not only for whores but for some high-class women as well. This led to constant fights between men to the amusement of the crowd. Food was sold outside in stores located near the main entrance and the spectators ate and often came early for good seats, sleeping stretched out over several of them. Since it was first come first served, this also led to fights. Antonio also told me a funny story about Divus Augustus, who loved the Circus. Augustus complained to an aristocrat who had brought his lunch, saying lunch was only to be eaten at home. The aristocrat had the nerve to retort that Augustus didn't have to worry about someone taking his seat!

Like our Hippodrome at home, the racing ground for the chariots is divided down the center into two tracks by a low wall. The short-end turns are so sharp that Antonio said almost every day one or two charioteers were killed making the turns or crashing into each other, and few live longer than to their midtwenties.

Antonio is a fanatic partisan of one of the four teams, the Greens. Each of the four has a color, Red, White, Green, and Blue. They wear their color on the harness of the horses and the chariot sides. That way their fans can identify them from a distance.

The day we went twenty charioteers were racing. It was thrilling. They lashed their horses at the start and shot forward like arrows. The crowd was screaming the names of their favorites. "Come on, come on, Green!" shouted Antonio while a man sitting near us snarled, "Go to the devil." He added, "I'm for the Reds." Antonio spit on the floor and shouted, "Damn the Red, Blue, and White teams! Go on, Green!"

The chariots whirled round the end posts of the separation wall, the Red driver smashing into the canal in a too-wide curve, and Antonio glanced triumphantly at the stranger, who sullenly looked down. Then the Blue charioteer, to the shrieking of the crowd, struck the separation wall as he approached the turn, flipped, and, with the horses loudly neighing, lay still. He was obviously dead. Some of the crowd groaned; others cheered.

The first course was over. I thought we might leave soon but Antonio was just starting to enjoy himself. "Go, go, Green!" he shrieked to the charioteer as the next chariot showing his color leaped forward when the rope dropped. "Ten denarii if you win. All for you," he shouted down. A young woman of what seemed respectable looks turned from a seat near us, smiled, and said, "I'll do it for ten denarii. Show me what's inside your toga." Those around us laughed, even the supporter of the Red team. "I've got a hundred denarii on Crescens," Antonio, who seemed to know the names of most of the charioteers, whispered to me. "If he wins, I'll treat you tonight to a *lupanaria*, which, Marcus, is a high-class brothel open twenty-four hours. And Marcus, Crescens won! Antonio was so excited he kissed me on both cheeks, got up, and shouted AVE CAESAR TIBERIUS, a clever pun on my name as his friend and that as well of the emperor. Spontaneously several other persons rose and stretched forward their right arms in the royal salute. It was a great moment.

The day flew by. I had brought dried figs, grapes, small bread rolls, and a bottle of *mulsum* white wine mixed with honey, and we ate the food and drank the wine. In the twenty races that day three charioteers died from crashes. It's a deadly sport. But the Romans love it. And of course slaves drive, so who cares!

Your brother, Tiberius

XI

I arrived back in Alexandria to learn that Emperor Tiberius at seventy-nine had at last died and Gaius Julius Germanicus was the new emperor. Rumor on the highest level was that the old emperor had a fainting fit while with Gaius, and the young man smothered him with a pillow or blanket. The surviving son of Germanicus, the most idealized Roman general, Gaius was called Caligula by everyone because while a boy on the frontier of Germania with his father he wore miniature military boots, or *caligae*.

We Jews of Alexandria had high hopes because one of Caligula's best friends from youth was Herod Agrippa of Judaea, now appointed king of Judaea by Caligula, and who had indeed been imprisoned previously by Tiberius for expressing the hope at an unguarded moment that Caligula would shortly become emperor.

We soon needed high-court Roman friends because what followed was one of the worst riots in Jewish history at Alexandria. The reason was odd. Emperor Tiberius toward the end of his long reign appointed his old friend Aulus Avilius Flaccus as praefectus, or governor of Egypt. All went well for five years and indeed Uncle Philo was an admirer of Flaccus. But an abrupt change came with the accession of Caligula, who disliked our praefectus due to the fact Flaccus had made a bad choice, openly preferring Tiberius Gemellus, cousin of Caligula, for emperor.

Flaccus, anxious to retain such a coveted post, conceived a clever idea. He issued an edict that all Jews must set up in their houses of worship statues of Caligula as divine, and he further proclaimed that all legal action be sworn to in the name of the divinity of the emperor. What worsened the problem, because no Jew could do these, was that the new emperor had a serious illness (probably caused by an overdose of a love potion) which impaired his brain and made him imagine that he was truly a god. A similar decree in Judaea created an even more serious crisis, the threat of wholesale rebellion in the province.

A massacre of the Jews by Flaccus for noncompliance to these decrees, which he called *conteminere deos*, or scorning god, was well planned. First he ordered all Jews in Alexandria into the Delta quarter; they had become so numerous that they lived in the Alpha quarter as well, two of the five quarters of Alexandria. The crowding as a result was so intense in the Delta that we were squeezed into all the public spaces, buildings, and even the tombs. Flaccus arrested the Jewish *gerousia*, or local governing body, beating the members severely. Several who had resisted arrest were crucified. Then Flaccus distributed weapons from the public arsenal to the Greek males, announcing that the Jews were "foreigners" with no legal rights.

The Greeks at this queue attacked the Delta quarter, sparing neither men, women, nor children. Since it was impossible in many cases to tell a Jew from a Greek (and intermarriage made it even more difficult), every male was forced to expose his genitals to see if he were circumcised; if not, he was let free; if so, he was viciously beaten or burned over wood fires. A rather curious result was that Egyptian priests, who had to be circumcised, were attacked as though Jews. The women were told to eat pork; if so they were freed; if they refused they were beaten or raped, both in the cases of young women. Then the Greeks sacked the houses, stealing everything of value. The loss of life was in the many thousands. The property loss was tremendous.

What Flaccus failed to realize were two things. First was the close friendship of Emperor Caligula and Herod Agrippa, dating back to childhood. Agrippa, now king of Judaea, it was claimed had a stroke on hearing the news. A very shrewd man, he hurried to Rome and reminded the emperor that Flaccus had opposed his elevation, preferring Caligula's cousin Tiberius Gemellus, who Caligula killed as soon as he attained power. An equally important point Agrippa brought up was that the Alexandrian riots had stopped the flow of grain to Rome, with great discontent on the part of the Roman populace because the public distributions were suspended. The final personal touch brought to Caligula's attention, through Agrippa as well, was the Egyptian Jews had passed a decree at his coming to power greatly honoring him; and this decree had been deliberately withheld by Flaccus.

The praefecture's fate was sealed. Flaccus was suspended from office, sent to the remote island of Andros, and there killed.

Our family had escaped attack because influential Greek friends had warned us of the preparations, and we shipped our most precious possessions to the south where we owned extensive property and then spent the period of the riots there.

That, however, was not the end of the story caused by Flaccus's miscalculation, for the Greeks of Alexandria, fearing a large assessment because of their rioting and destruction of property, sent a delegation of their most distinguished citizens to justify their action before Caligula. This forced the Alexandrian Jews to send a similar delegation to confute the Greeks, a delegation headed by my Uncle Philo and including my father as well.

In two works by Philo, *In Flaccum* (On Flaccus) and *Legatio ad Gaium* (The Embassy to Gaius), the former dealt with the atrocities committed by the Greeks instigated by Flaccus and the latter described the two delegations sent to the emperor.

During all this terrible time I had returned and was safely settled at Thebes in the south. There were few Greeks there and we were protected by our Nubian employees. It was through reading what my uncle wrote that I learned the details.

Emperor Caligula decided to delay seeing the two delegations and in typical fashion left both fuming while he visited Gallia and then passed the summer on an estate in Campania, South Italy. It was over a year before he returned to Rome and received the two delegations, both of which had spent large sums of money to influence his advisors.

Receiving the Jewish delegation first, Caligula said, "So you are a people who won't eat pig," at which his courtiers exploded in laughter. Then, gritting his teeth, he sneered, "So you are the god-haters who do not believe I am a god."

The Jews proclaimed their loyalty and insisted they sacrificed to ensure the emperor's well-being.

"What good is that? You have not sacrificed to me as a god!" Caligula exclaimed.

The Jews at this point with some success turned the discussion in another direction and cleverly emphasized that the riots and general disorder were due to Flaccus, who they knew that Caligula had hated. He calmed down and finally said, "I think these men are not so much criminals as lunatics," and, after hearing the Greek delegation, dismissed both.

Shortly thereafter, with growing lunacy and erratic behavior, Caligula was assassinated by members of the *praetoriani*, the imperial guards, and Claudius became emperor. There is no question, however, that Caligula's friendship from childhood with Agrippa, and the latter's intercession behind the scenes (with the still more dangerous crisis for the same reason in Judaea, namely worship of Caligula as a god) was a vital factor. Otherwise the Judean war would have broken out more than twenty-five years earlier. My Uncle Philo, in his above-mentioned writings, rather ascribed the happy ending to divine providence: first Flaccus and then Caligula were stricken down by Yahweh.

It seemed not only the Jews of Alexandria were secure, but also that our family was touched by divine blessing. Business was going well. Marcus turned out to be very clever and my father was delighted. In fact, the Alexandrian Jews never had it better; Emperor Claudius, who followed Caligula, issued a strong warning of dire action if either Jews or Greeks would riot. And then came the crowning glory, the marriage of my brother Marcus to Princess Berenice, the daughter of King Agrippa of Judaea, uniting what was considered the richest Jewish family of Egypt, our family, to the royal house of Judaea.

XII

It is worth noting a bit of the history of Herod Agrippa, an amazing man. He was often referred to as Agrippa I because his son bore the same name and was thus called Agrippa II.

Agrippa was the grandson of Herod the Great and son of Aristobulus by Herod's wife Mariamne, a beautiful Hasmonean princess. Mariamne and her sons, Aristobulus and Alexander, were killed by Herod in his delusions of conspiracy—Herod killed eight of his sons by ten wives. But his grandson Agrippa was spared because Mariamne was of priestly Jewish stock and thus was thought of by Herod as a source of continued family dynastic rule.

Imperial Roman policy was to bring to Rome at a young age the male heirs of the kings who were their high-class pawns, and treat them intimately and in close contact with their nobility so that in the future they would admire Roman culture and accept subservient rule. Agrippa was thus sent to Rome at about the age of five and brought up with heirs to the throne, where he became specially friendly with young Caligula. Since Julius Caesar had adopted Herod into the Julio-Claudian line, as was our family by Augustus, he was considered a high aristocrat.

Spending all the family's money in riotous living and broke, Agrippa was forced to leave Rome. Moving from place to place through family contacts, he finally came to my father and requested a large loan. Father was somewhat in awe of the grandson of Herod and the royal Hasmonean Mariamne and particularly admired

Agrippa's wife Kypros who, unlike her husband, was a deeply observant Jewess. Father lent him the money on the condition that while Agrippa went to Rome to see the Emperor Tiberius, his wife Kypros and their three children would go back to Judaea to raise the children as good Jews. This Kypros did. One of the children was Berenice who, as I will now relate, became the wife of my brother Marcus.

Then Agrippa made a mistake out of his extraordinary ambition which almost cost him his life. With Caligula the heir apparent to be Roman emperor, he expressed the hope, as I formerly noted, that Caligula would soon become emperor, i.e., that Tiberius would die or be killed. This was reported to the emperor, who promptly clapped Agrippa into jail.

Fate has its tricks. Tiberius died—most probably killed—shortly thereafter and Caligula, now emperor, had his friend Agrippa released and not only loaded him with gifts but bestowed on him the kingdom of Judaea, as it had been that of his grandfather Herod. This was the man who toppled Flaccus and restored order and tranquility again to the Jews of Alexandria. Indeed, Agrippa lived only three years as a very popular king of Judaea before dying. If longer, the fate of Judaea might have been very different.

XIII

As I dictate to Isocrates, my learned Greek slave, tears come to my eyes and run down the remains of my nose. We never know destiny, good or bad, and changes can happen like flashes of lightning. It happened to us, to our family.

But to proceed. The wedding of my brother Marcus to Princess Berenice, his child bride—she was only thirteen—took place on the spacious grounds of the great *proseuche*. "Everyone came": the new praefectus of Egypt; the commanders of the 5th and 10th legions stationed in our country as well as their officers; Alexandria's city officials; several Roman noblemen who were in Egypt on state business, purple straps showing vividly on their mantles; and the rector and top librarians of the Great Library, friends of Uncle Philo. I was amused to see my father's Nubian commander of the troops from the warehouses at Koptos. He hung in a corner too embarrassed or afraid to speak to such luminaries but ate his fill of sweet cakes and drank so much red wine that I thought as the evening went on he would turn red from black. An emissary through a megaphone even read a scroll expressing the good wishes of Emperor Claudius, our new emperor after Caligula had been killed. And through the crowd, hand in hand, wandered Princess Berenice and my brother Marcus receiving applause or dodging nuts thrown at them, an old Roman custom. And also Roman custom, the bride was wearing an elaborately knitted girdle and a saffron veil which hid her lovely young face.

My father and King Agrippa of Judaea had spared no expense, the latter of course being the father of the bride. I couldn't believe my eyes; even a Parthian prince came to the celebration. I noticed that he and King Agrippa went off for a long talk in a quiet corner.

The event began with a huge elephant sauntering through the crowd. On his back was perched his trainer. Behind the trainer was framed a large four-sided box. In purple letters on all four sides against a white background was painted AMOR PATRIAE. The crowd roared. One of the Roman noblemen shouted AVE CAESAR. The great majority took up the chant AVE CAESAR, AVE CAESAR CLAUDIUS, though I did note a few persons with closed mouths.

Next came a supersized synthetic donkey on whose sides were painted CARPE DIEM, that is, "Seize the day," or enjoy, which particularly pleased the crowd because where his tail should have been was a spigot, and when a slave turned the spigot out ran red wine of the best Mareotis vintage, which he caught in glasses from a side panel and handed out to the eager guests. Inside the donkey was another slave who through open slats repeated in a loud voice again and again CARPE DIEM. For those who desired beer, the popular and tasty Henket was available in large pitchers. A special table was set aside on whose top were casks of the finest vintage of Setininian and Falerian wine; one of my father's most trusted slaves was in charge at the table and warned to give glasses of those wines to men with purple straps on their mantles only, that is, the visiting Roman aristocrats, as well of course to the praefectus of Egypt and his high staff. As for the few ladies who didn't drink wine, they were offered tart pomegranate juice.

Following the synthetic donkey with the wine spigot came the introduction to the meal. A large round pot on an enormous silver plate was brought in, carried by four slaves, with what seemed a baked paste crust. The slaves deposited the plate and each took out a dagger, slitting the four corners of the crust. Out flew, tripping over each other in their haste, a flock of doves. The crowd applauded wildly.

The last part of the preliminaries to the meal was a troupe of monkeys, tails tied together and led by a trainer, who circled them round the grounds. Hanging from their necks were signs painted in purple: VIVAT MARCUS, VIVAT BERENICE.

The sumptuous meal was almost an afterthought, for most of the guests were already reeling from the wine. Hundreds of silver or woven papyrus baskets, at least one-half meter round, were placed on the tables set along the wide lawn, all filled with different delicacies: dry Egyptian dates, sweet Damascus figs, filberts, walnuts, cheeses, fruits, coconut slices, boiled eggs, olives, pickles, gourds, and barley cakes. Other baskets had heartier fare: shredded chicken, thrush, duck, and many varieties of tarts and cookies. Containers of olive oil, salt, and herbs were placed alongside the salad bowls holding asparagus and chopped salted fish.

Of course no pig products or shell fish were served, but to compensate there were baskets of ice to cool the wine, which had been shipped in special sealed jugs from Britannia, it already being winter there. And the few vegetarians were offered raw seasoned vegetables with fish-pickle dip. For dessert there was chilled *dulcia domestica*—pitted dates stuffed with dried fruit, nuts, cake crumbs, and spices—all dipped in wine. And small groups of actors wandered among the crowd either singing popular songs or reciting amatory verses from Horace, Catullus, and Ovid.

The event lasted into the night and when it ended the large lawn was sprinkled with drunks too far gone to go home. It was a spectacular wedding spoken about for many years.

Black shadows rose with my father shortly thereafter. Due to the influence of family friends I had received a state job involving customs liaison where I worked with the military at Elephantine in South Egypt, incidentally aiding my brother, who operated nearby. This position, technically military but really administrative, required nothing more than the usual military oath: "I swear to perform with enthusiasm whatever the Emperor commands, never to desert, and not shrink from death on behalf of the Roman state." This of course I could take without difficulty because there was no statement as to the divinity of the emperor.

The problem came up, however, when Emperor Claudius in his initial year, probably through the suggestion of his mother, "Auntie Antonia," who had liked me on my visit to Rome, offered to advance me to the position of epistrategus of the Thebaid. This was a kind of municipal governor of the most southern of the three regions of Egypt. Because of our connections I would not have to go through the usual *tres militae*, a military training required for a knightly career. My duties would be the minimum though the prestige was great, and they involved juridical decisions that required mere common sense and various community duties.

The problem, however, was that now I had to swear an oath which proclaimed the divinity of the emperor, which no Jew could take. My brother Marcus, who spent every other week at our warehouses in Koptos while his wife Berenice lived with our parents, urged me not to take the oath, which would be apostasy, but rather join him in the family business. On the other hand, if I would become epistrategus of the south where we had our entry point for goods from the East, I could obviously benefit greatly the family fortune.

I was at a turnstile. Unlike Marcus I was no believer in the Judaic rites and despite my father's anger, hadn't attended a *proseuche* in years. On the other hand the thought of officially disavowing my Jewish background was not an easy thing to do despite my love for all things Roman.

I went home and spoke with father and Uncle Philo. They were horrified. From my studies at the Alexandrian Library I pointed out the long and honorable military history of the Jews in Egypt: the Jewish military colony at Elephantine serving the Ptolemies in remote times; the Jewish general Dositheos under Ptolemy VI; the two Jews, Hellkias and Ananias, who were commanders-in-chief of the army of Cleopatra III. I must admit that I was proud of my knowledge; I had reviewed this history before seeing my father and uncle.

No use. Father may not have known the history but my uncle did. "Tiberius," he said, "don't play games with us. Under the Ptolemies anyone who spoke Koinē was a Hellene regardless of his origins. But this is no longer true. A Greek of Greek origin is a Greek Egyptian. A Jew who speaks Koinē is a Jewish Egyptian. And you know in both cases that is inferior for the Romans. Our family is Roman by adoption, among the few Egyptians who are Romans, because of your father's financial aid to Octavius before he became Emperor Augustus. And so we don't even pay the Roman poll tax. But these military figures you spoke of, and you are correct in what you say, were under the Ptolemies and not the Romans. They were Hellenes, not Egyptians. So what you say has no import."

I tried another approach. "The oath of divinity to the emperor is almost without meaning," I claimed. "It is simply a way of gluing together the different peoples of the empire by a common allegiance. Why, when Emperor Tiberius died the delighted Roman mobs ran through the streets breaking off the heads of his marble statues. Do you think they would do that if they believed in his divinity? The oath is a formality and nothing more. In fact," I added, "I hear the sculptors now sculpt the bodies of an emperor leaving a hole where the head goes, and with each new emperor they thus can make a new head, remove the old one, and insert in the empty hole the new emperor's head attached to a peg. Some divinity!"

That meant nothing to my father. "*Theos megalos*, Great Yahweh is the One who is. I have listened for years to my brother Philo comparing the prophets of Judaea to Greek philosophers as though they are more or less the same. He even told me the two of you went to hear some fool claiming to be a Jew who said that a certain Yeshua in Judaea had announced that he was part of Yahweh or son of Yahweh or some stupid thing like that. But there is only one truth and that is, 'Hear O Israel, the Lord our Yahweh, the lord is one!' And the teacher He sent was Moses. All else is apostasy. And as to apostasy it is also said, 'They sleep in Gehenna, hell, forever; they have no share in the life to come.' Sometimes I even think my brother Philo trembles on the edge of apostasy when he claims the sole truth comes from the Mosaic Scriptures, ignoring the great oral traditions and clarifications of the Judean rabbis."

"And the chosen people are the Judeans?" I asked. "The Judeans, who occupy a tiny corner of the Great Sea and who, moreover, seem to fight with each other more than with non-Judeans? *They* are the Chosen People, chosen by Yahweh, not the Romans who have conquered almost the whole world and who put up with the Judean squabbling solely because that province is a bumper west of the Parthian Empire. And if we are the Chosen People, why did Joseph, Moses, David, and Solomon marry non-Judean women? And how about Ruth, the ancestress of King David?"

"And so you are resolved to take the oath of divinity for the emperor?" My father's face was bloodshot.

"With my mouth, not my heart."

"Not good enough. You leave our people if you take the oath. You become an apostate."

"So be it!" I said in fury. And going to my old room I packed a few essentials and stormed out of our family mansion. It was the last time I saw my parents or Uncle Philo.

I rose in the world—I will describe how—and my family went down as though there was an adverse relation. "Auntie Antonia" gave the Egyptian property as a wedding present to her daughter, whose husband, a profligate aristocrat, promptly sold it to another Egyptian who removed my father as administrator. The family was reduced in wealth. But the real disaster came shortly thereafter.

It had become a custom to celebrate the emperor's birthday with feasts throughout the empire. They took place naturally at Alexandria as well, and to the festivities were invited by the praefectus and his staff the high-ranking officers of the two legions stationed in Egypt. That left the 5th legion camp at Elephantine without formal leadership. The legionnaires as well celebrated the imperial occasion. They came back from the Nile outposts to their headquarters at Elephantine and got royally drunk.

The desert Arabs on the other side of the Nile took advantage of this opportunity and hundreds strong crossed the Nile, invaded our family warehouses at Koptos, stealing all the merchandise and killing the Nubian guards. My brother Marcus, staying at nearby Thebes on business, rushed to the scene to rally the remaining Nubians, who took flight. Marcus was struck by an arrow in the chest, and without a doctor to help him, bled to death. In one night another good part of the family fortune was wiped out and my brother Marcus was killed.

I went home on hearing the news, to be rebuffed at the door. The only person who would see me was Berenice, now a widow while still a young adolescent. She cracked open the door, eyes bloodshot from crying, pallid, dressed in black. "Go away," she said. "Nobody wants to see you, you Roman hireling." She spit out the words. "I can tell you one thing. Your father said he wished it had been Tiberius instead."

Those words I never can forget. There is not a month of my life when I do not dream of my father leaning over me and saying, "I wish it were you instead of Marcus." But it seemed like there was a genie who spied on the family, pushing me up while the rest went down.

XIV

It was a scorching day in southern Egypt and I lay prostate on my bed when a knock came at the door. "Who is it?" I called out, annoyed, and motioned to my Nubian houseboy to stop waving a large fan at the head of my bed.

"A message from the Emperor Claudius," said a voice I recognized as Roman.

I struggled to my feet, slipped on short pants, and went to the door. Outside stood a centurion from the 5th legion.

I was stunned. What could I have done? Could my father have protested to Emperor Claudius through "Auntie" Antonia, his mother, my mother's close friend? No, ridiculous; that far my father wouldn't go.

I opened the door. "Yes?" I inquired of the centurion.

He handed me a sealed parchment holding a small scroll, extended his right arm in the royal salute, turned, mounted his horse, and rode off.

The scroll was very short. "To Epistrategus Tiberius Julius Alexander. Come to Rome immediately. Your Emperor."

Though the heat was intense, a cold shiver ran down my back. What could this message mean? I had visited Emperor Claudius short months ago on routine Egyptian business and he'd been very friendly. I remember he quipped, "You and I are among the few Julio-Claudians who like only women!" Indeed, he tried to get me to marry a highborn Roman lady. I rejected his suggestion politely, saying I was devoting my life solely for the good of the Roman Empire. But the truth was that I had vowed never again to suffer through love as I had suffered with Penelope, fearing the power of a woman over me, as I had that of my father's domination when I was young. It was far easier to go to a beautiful whore, pay, and then forget her.

So what had I done wrong? What did the emperor want from me? But on further thought, his signing "Your Emperor" did not seem menacing.

Of course a call from the emperor preceded everything. I dressed, called my assistant, and reviewed current problems, giving him written authority to act while I was away. I then took a four-horse chariot to arrive quickly at Alexandria, boarding the first boat of our flotilla leaving for Ostia, Rome's new main port.

Requesting an audience with the emperor after washing and a change of clothes, I was met by his dreaded minister, the freedman Narcissus, a man with a ruthless reputation. He was very friendly, however, and I relaxed, even more so when he dismissed the two guards without telling them to search me.

"How goes it with our Egyptian friend?" Narcissus asked with a smile.

"A Roman from Egypt," I said.

Narcissus laughed. "Right. Our Roman friend, a Roman Julio-Claudian from Egypt. I stand corrected. Tiberius Julius," he added, skipping the Alexander.

I bowed my head. It was wiser not to duel words with Narcissus.

"The emperor will receive you. He has been informed you arrived in Rome." He opened the inner door.

Emperor Claudius was sitting in loose clothing on a casual arm-chair. He was a handsome man, well-built, with a shock of white hair, his belly bulging through the informal dress, the belly of most Roman noblemen from drinking too much red wine.

I will try to recall the conversation, though of course it was many years ago. I will omit most of the stammering and slobbering, the drooling and jerking, which accompanied our emperor and for which reason no one could explain except for some fancy theories of certain doctors.

"Welcome to Rome." Claudius turned to Narcissus. "Take notes on the talk. You are part of what I have to say."

Narcissus nodded and took out a stylus and parchment pad.

"You know of course, Tiberius," he said with a friendly gesture, "of that stupid rebellion of Furius Camillus Scribonianus in Dalmatia last year."

"Of course," I said. "And he wasn't even a Julio-Claudian."

The emperor roared with laughter, spittle flowing from his mouth. "Did you hear that, Narcissus? Not even a Julio-Claudian. Tiberius has a good sense of humor."

Narcissus laughed. I was astonished. He even winked at me.

"Of course that damn fool was eliminated by my loyal centurions. Not before, however, Narcissus succeeded by some—what shall we say, some adroit methods—to make Scribonianus reveal the names of fourteen knights and seven senators who conspired with him."

"And they too are no longer with us," the emperor added, nodding at Narcissus.

"To continue," the emperor said, his nose dripping. "This is still a secret but I am planning an invasion of Britannia. The island is a sore in my throat. The Druids there are always stirring up trouble in Gallia. Our great Julius Caesar wrote of them and their filthy habits, banishing them from Gallia. But I'm told they slip over from Britannia to Gallia and try to rouse the people against us."

"I've read Caesar's *Commentarii de bello Gallico*," I said. "The Druids offer human sacrifices and burn living persons in wicker cages. They have a custom of burying a small child in the foundation of new buildings and sacrifice youths during their spring rites."

"Who cares what the Druids do," Narcissus said. "Our Roman traders tell me that the island has large mines of tin, lead, and silver, as well as pearls."

"And beautiful women," the emperor added and laughed, wiping the drip from his nose.

I sat silent. How did I fit into all this?

As though the emperor read my mind, he turned to me.

"My mother tells me that your family is the most loyal in Egypt and she personally has trusted your father with the management of all her Egyptian property for decades."

I smiled and said nothing, hoping fervently that the emperor was not aware of the new developments as to his mother's property and also my family quarrel.

Apparently not, for Claudius continued.

"I need someone absolutely loyal to me for an important mission. And I've decided that you are the ideal person."

I nodded, not daring to speak.

"The only senior commander I have available for the invasion of Britannia is Aulus Plautius, commander of the 9th legion. But he comes from a very noble family—my first wife was a Plautia, Plautia Urganilla, whom I divorced for her wild sexual conduct—and I don't trust any of those high noblemen. I do have faith in Titus Flavius Vespasianus, commander of the 2nd legion, but he is too young for the supreme command. I want you to work with him."

I knew the name—Vespasianus, called Vespasian by everyone—was a few years older than I and had advanced rapidly in the military due to his courage and ability. But what appealed to the emperor most, I thought, was Vespasian's plebeian birth and therefore no threat.

"And what would be my role?" I asked.

"I have no reason to distrust Commander Aulus Plautius, but Narcissus has recommended my being on guard. After all, he will be in supreme command of four legions, his 9th from Pannonia and three from the Rhine—the 2nd under Vespasianus, the 14th, and the 20th. With cavalry and many auxiliaries, he will be in command of some 40,000 soldiers. That's a large force.

"Narcissus has suggested we appoint you *praefectus castra*, or post commander, responsible for the activities of the 2nd legion, in this case a spy under Vespasianus in control of the courier relay to Narcissus at Rome. We cannot use the beacon-light system, though it is of course much quicker, because anyone can read those simple signals. You will report once a week any suspicious activities, any hints of disloyalty, if necessary even bypassing General Vespasian himself. The courier will report directly to you—you will make up some plausible reason to allay suspicions—and you will notify us of any disloyal activity. Narcissus will provide you code to be used. Memorize it and then chew it up and swallow it."

I remained breathless and wordless for seconds. Then I spoke.

"Oh, my emperor, oh Emperor Claudius, what an honor. Oh, what an honor!" I continued, "I need not thank you, my emperor, the honor is beyond thanks. I will be crucified before I say a word to anyone or betray the distinction bestowed upon me."

I thought quickly. The situation was ripe for my suggesting some ideas that could help my career. "May I suggest two things?" I asked.

"Yes," said Claudius, "Go ahead."

"We spoke of the Druids. They are strong in Britannia and are our avowed enemies. Julius Caesar in his book on their customs wrote that they were said to outlaw anyone who embraced the Roman religion. He also wrote that the Druid priests painted themselves blue with a marsh plant called woad when performing their religious rites or going to war with the Gallic troops.

"What I suggest is that we instruct archers to shoot at any person painted blue. This would cause panic in their army and also get rid of a mortal enemy."

"Good point," said the emperor. "Be sure to take that down, Narcissus. And what is your other point?"

"Recently I spoke to one of our traders who had come to Egypt to buy emeralds. He told me that there's an upheaval in Britannia, where he had just come back from. You of course know that in Britannia, king of Regnenses, Verica, was deposed by the king of the Catevellauni, his powerful neighbor, and Verica has fled to Rome and appealed for help."

"Of course I know. I support him. I saw him last week," said Claudius.

"Good. What I suggest is that we take Verica with our troops and make a side foray into Regnenses, toppling the Catevellauni invaders. Then, putting Verica back on his throne, we will have an important ally who will supply us with support troops."

"By Jupiter, what a clever idea," said Claudius. "Have you ever thought of joining the military, of becoming a military magistrate, a *tribunus militum*?"

"Very clever," mumbled Narcissus, fixing a cold eye on me.

That made me nervous. One knew better than to get on the wrong side of Narcissus. "I only propose those two ideas for the good of our glorious empire," I said. "For myself at your command I am happy to stay in Egypt, my native land."

"Enough," said Claudius. "Narcissus has written down your ideas. Stay in Rome at my expense. I'll speak to Polybius, my freedman who takes care of such things. He'll arrange everything. And Narcissus will give you the code for our contact. Settle your affairs in Egypt and prepare to move north through Gallia within a month."

That is my best recollection of an event that changed my life. Of course the next thing I did was to look up my dear friend Antonio Julius Lepidus, only to be told that he had been appointed a centurion, as I knew he would, and sent east of Dalmatia. I sent the news to my assistant in the Thebaid, giving him the authority to act in my prolonged absence. Then I spent a month, I don't remember how, dicing, whoring, drinking, going to the Circus Maximus, the theatre, or just walking for amusement along the Tiber and the Palatine, Rome's seat of government. The time passed quickly. Polybius sent me more money than I needed and Narcissus provided the code, which I promptly memorized and then chewed up.

The trip north through Gallia was likewise uneventful. We were a small group, mainly merchants; Emperor Claudius did not want to arouse any suspicions. In fact King Verica went separately in a more conspicuous convoy.

The three legions from the Rhine and the one from the Danube met and pitched camp at Boulogne, a small town at the most narrow point of the channel between Gallia and Britannia. It was an awesome sight. Some 24,000 legionnaires, almost an equal amount of auxiliary troops, cavalry, 5,000 horses, slaves to provide services for the army, and 400 transport ships, plus the naval vessels to protect the convoy. And of course the usual camp followers—whores, peddlers, beggars—were all dumped within weeks on a small seaside village. The inhabitants were at first terrified, and then delighted, as their food and wares doubled and then quadrupled in sale price. The few soldiers who spoke the native language, mainly volunteers from Gallia, became very popular with the town girls as well.

I met Vespasian, the general of the 2nd legion from the Rhine. He of course had been informed of my arrival and duties. We became friends almost immediately, calling each other by first names. And we were close in age, which bonded us.

As my close relation with Vespasian, the future emperor, changed my life completely, I will add a few comments as to the man himself. Vespasian was of middle height, fair of skin, with a thick face, a hooked nose and prominent chin. He was not ashamed of his plebeian birth, spoke simply and to the point, and was given to ribald soldier's talk and jesting. He had a reputation of fairness and honesty, which was true for him all his life.

My attempt at secrecy, which I rigorously kept, was useless with Vespasian, who well knew that an Egyptian would not have been elevated to the position of *praefectus castra*, and especially a person of my age, unless there was a deeper reason. At first he thought I had been placed to watch him but, shrewd by nature, he soon realized that there was another reason. At all times, and even during the invasion itself, he gave me full and honest reports of what went on at the meetings of the general staff, including Commander Aulus Plautius as well.

The problem I reported to Narcissus was not related to the generals. It had to do with the soldiers themselves, especially those coming from the Rhine. The three legions had been stationed there for many years. They were bunked in comfortable quarters, with shops, cheap wine, and easy activities. It was illegal for legionnaires to marry but most of them—young and vigorous men—had illicit relations and even children. Although the centurions were almost all Roman or from Italian territory, many of the enlisted men were from the German-speaking areas, and their relations with the Germans in the Rhine as well as the Danube were friendly, as though neighbors and not conquerors. After their service was up, still rather young, they married German women, had children, and raised their children to become legionnaires in turn.

These soldiers bitterly resented being uprooted from their comfortable lives and sent on short notice to Gallia to invade a hostile island across a treacherous sea, and to a land noted for its brave warriors, where many of them of course would be killed. This strong feeling was shared as well by most of the centurions, whose lifestyle was even more comfortable.

Although the invasion had been scheduled for April, violent storms on the channel held up the debarkation. This left the army, with nothing to do, even more restless. General Vespasian told me that even some of his centurions had verged on being insolent, questioning the new emperor's intelligence—Claudius was still considered by many as little more than an idiot. I felt impelled to report the almost-mutinous behavior. I sent a dispatch to Narcissus describing the situation and suggesting the emperor appear to appease the troops. By return dispatch, within ten days, the answer arrived. Narcissus himself would come as soon as possible with the emperor's word that decimation—killing every tenth soldier—or even crucifixion would be used to put down any attempted mutiny.

Narcissus at this time was rising to the zenith of power, already leading Claudius by the nose. Even Commander Aulus Plautius feared him: Narcissus was known to give death warrants to the emperor, who without reading signed them.

Quick in action, Narcissus called for a meeting of 180 centurions:

each of the three legions had about 6,000 men divided into ten cohorts and there were six centurions in each cohort. (The 9th Danubian legion, not mutinous, was excluded.) These men, the pick of the army, received a sharp reprimand. I was there, as of course were the legion generals, and—though that was many years ago—I will try to remember the gist of the speech, which was of course much longer.

Narcissus stood on a tribunal platform before the centurions. He was short, pudgy, and had a sharp aquiline face, with a short nose and skin toward the dark side. He was Greek by birth and spoke with an accent.

As I wrote, most of the centurions were Romans or from Italian territory. Looking at him, a few could not hold back. One called out "Greek" and another "freedman," while several hooted.

Narcissus flushed, his skin darker than ever. "All who don't want to hear, step forward. You know the fate of traitors. Step forward."

Naturally no one did.

"I come here as the representative of your emperor, Emperor Claudius, emperor of our great Roman Empire who you have sworn to defend and do whatever is required as part of that oath to the state. You did not join our army to live in luxury or sleep with German women or to have German bastards. Am I right or wrong? Speak up, speak up as Roman soldiers, as centurions."

A silence was followed by a few shouts and raising of arms in the royal salute. Others followed.

Commander Aulus Plautius stepped forward. "A cheer for Emperor Claudius and his royal representative, Narcissus." He turned to Narcissus and raised forward his right hand in salute. "To Narcissus, to the emperor. Long live Emperor Claudius."

The atmosphere was catching. Several older legionnaires came through the crowd, pushing aside their younger comrades. "To Inferno with traitors," one called out. "Decimate the bastards. Long live the emperor.

"Long live the emperor. Long live Emperor Claudius," he shouted again.

Narcissus smiled. "I have been instructed by our emperor to give 100 gold aureii to each centurion when we return."

Delirium broke out, whistles, shouts, the centurions pounding each others' shoulders.

The incipient revolt ended. There were no more complaints reported despite what the ordinary soldiers may have felt. Iron discipline was the order again.

The weather cleared. We disembarked in June. The fleet was a glorious sight. Each of the transports carried two hundred soldiers, or fifty soldiers and fifty horses, as well of course the sailors and rowers. The convoy protectors, or fighting ships, were long and wide, propelled by two banks of oars. They carried throwing projectiles and specially trained marines expert in archery. As I watched aboard the royal transport, the Roman eagles of the four legions held high, the soldiers cheering, the flags flapping, I felt again, as I had in youth, that the Roman Empire was not only glorious but was destined to live forever, and that those who opposed it deserved to be crushed. I write this now because it was an important factor in my later actions as a very high Roman military general.

Commander Aulus Plautius knew his main enemy would be the powerful Catevellauni tribe, with the Regnenses friendly (deposed King Verica was with us), while the other, less powerful tribes, would probably sway back and forth depending who showed the most strength. Three separate landings took place directly in Catevellauni territory in order to break their strength as soon as possible.

I did no fighting. I only carried a stiff metal buckler for protection, but what I did was far more important for my future career. I observed the tactics of Commander Plautius, a seasoned veteran of many wars, as well as those of General Vespasian, with whom I camped. And I learned. It is one thing to read about military tactics, as I did when young, and quite another to participate in wars.

Togodumnus and Caractacus, brothers and dual kings of the Catevellauni, had brought their joint forces to the far bank of the Medway River, close to the channel, as a defense barrier. They were unused to Roman skill in forging rivers, as well as dealing with enemy chariots. At nightfall Commander Plautius threw across the Medway River German auxiliaries adept at swimming while fully armed. Once across, under instructions, they attacked not the enemy soldiers but rather cut the tendons of the war-chariot horses. The frantic neighing of the horses, unable to stand, the upsetting of the chariots, the confusion of their drivers, the general disorder, permitted the main body of the Roman troops, who had assembled together, to cross the river.

Then, as night fell and the Britains slept, Plautius sent over our 2nd legion, commanded by Vespasian with me as an observer, to move south along the river and, finding a ford, to attack the flank of the enemy at daybreak.

About two miles down we found a ford and in the pitch black the troops silently waded to the other side. Vespasian was amazing. Most generals would have taken a short nap while the soldiers crossed. Not Vespasian. He stood thigh-deep in the running water while encouraging the men, calling soldiers by name and joking with the centurions. Only after the entire legion had crossed did he follow.

Our legion attacked at dawn. The Britains, totally unprepared to see the enemy charge—6,000 strong plus auxiliaries—in the dim morning light, broke ranks. Then by prearrangement the full force of the other three legions frontally attacked, trumpets blaring, soldiers shouting. Togodumnus was killed; his brother Caractacus, surrounded by a rear-guard, left the field and, as we later learned, disappeared into the wild mountains of Wales.

With this one single battle the forces of Britannia's strongest tribe were broken and there was no longer any single foe on the entire island capable of opposing us. Our loss of life in the battle was little, though thirty new centurions had to be promoted from the top fighting men for those killed. King Verica, our valiant Regnenses tribal king, was also killed by an enemy archer when our troops first crossed the Medway River.

It was estimated from captives that the enemy forces at the Medway amounted to some 60,000 men, almost double our legionnaires, but superior Roman strategy had won the battle. However, it did take four more years of sporadic fighting to occupy all the southwestern part of the central island, the civilized part, and organize the new province of Britannia.

Commander Plautius was right in not splitting our forces by a foray into Regnenses territory, as I had suggested. Nor could we use my other suggestion, to kill the Druids painted blue, because they were not yet awake when we attacked. Instead, Plautius had been correct to concentrate his legions, inferior in number, and strike with his total force in one decisive battle. I repeat, I was learning.

As a clever commander and one cautious for his own skin when any misstep might mean loss of his life under a despotic regime, Aulus Plautius insisted Emperor Claudius toward the end of the campaign come to the island to participate at the finish of serious fighting and thus claim a Triumph for himself. The emperor came. He traveled by sea from Ostia with his staff to Massilia, the major southern seaport of Gallia, and then was carried in a light sedan to Boulogne, where he took a transport across the channel. Protected securely behind our lines, he attended the last decisive battle, the capture of Comulodunum, the enemy capital.

I was not at that battle nor did I attend the Triumph at Rome. When it was obvious that I was no longer needed, Narcissus ordered me back to the capital. Unlike my last visit I was kept waiting three months for an audience with the emperor, who had taken a vacation from the summer heat to stay at Capri, noted for its balmy climate. I was very irritated but there was nothing for me to do. I requested an audience with Narcissus, but he was with the emperor. I ran out of money but Polybius, still at Rome, told me he had received no orders to give me more. Then, apparently conveying my distress to Capri, the emperor released my wages as the epistrategus in the Egyptian Thebaid.

Finally October came. The emperor returned and in a week I

received word he would see me. Like before, Narcissus met me and like before I was not searched when entering the presence of the emperor. This was a high compliment, as I knew. In fact, Claudius smiled and waved a friendly hand.

"Welcome, Tiberius Julius Alexander." Then, perhaps realizing for the first time the oddity of a Roman Julio-Claudian with the name Alexander, Claudius quipped: "A descendant of Alexander the Great?"

"I'd prefer, like you, to be a descendant of Divus Augustus."

Claudius laughed and then, choking, spit into a large piss pot at his feet. "Now to business," he said, catching his breath. "Narcissus told me that Ethiopia is supposed to be rich in gold and ivory. Are you aware of that?"

"Of course, my emperor. In fact you own the most important gold mine close to the southern border of Egypt with Ethiopia, at the Wadi Allagi. *Wad* is river in the Egyptian language. The mine is under my supervision and all the gold is sent to you on the Nile by soldiers of the 5th legion."

Claudius looked at Narcissus. It was obvious he knew nothing of the gold mine. Narcissus nodded and added, "It's below Aswan, at the edge of the Nubian Desert."

"Oh," said the emperor, though it seemed apparent he was not aware of what we were talking about. "If Ethiopia's so rich, why don't we march in and take over the riches? Didn't I order the two legions in Egypt to do that? Or am I confusing them with the revolt in Mauretania?"

"No, you are right, as usual, about the two legions in Egypt," Narcissus said diplomatically. "But everything was put on hold, not only the putting down of the revolt in Mauretania but for the conquest of Britannia."

"Besides, as you of course know," I added though I was quite sure he didn't know, "Gaius Petronius, the third praefectus of Egypt for Divus Augustus, repelling an invasion from Ethiopia, counter-attacked and pursued the enemy up the Nile to Napata, taking their capital. But that happened about the same time that Arminius in Germania destroyed three of our legions, and Divus Augustus, appalled, ordered Gaius Petronius to evacuate the country in his decision to consolidate our empire."

"I remember that, I still remember that," said the emperor. "I was nineteen at the time and we were all terrified at the rage of Divus Augustus on losing under Commander Varus those three legions. But times have changed. The empire is stronger and richer now."

"True enough, especially under you," I said, and noting an ironic smile on Narcissus's face. I decided not to push the flattery too far.

"But we have another problem there that all our legions can't fight," I added.

"What is that?"

"Most of our traders in Ethiopia bring their wares to Adulis, their seaport. But that far south on the Nile, with no protection from our legions, there are many sea pirates. So some merchants come back inland to Egypt. I entertain them and try to learn what I can do to be of use if we go ahead with an invasion. And there is a more serious problem."

"Good-looking women who will seduce our soldiers?" Claudius joked. He took out a cotton cloth and wiped his dripping nose.

"A fly like our houseflies, called by the natives the tsetse. This fly is unknown in the Thebaid, which is desert. But once farther south of the First Cataract the land becomes more fertile, with marshes and lakes, and this is the habitat of the dreaded fly. It sucks human blood and causes what is known as sleeping sickness, a fever and wasting away, affecting horses and cattle as well. For the natives it is a chronic condition and is not too serious but for white men it is fatal. Our traders dread it more than robbers or pirates. And knowledge of the disease, which our 5th legionnaires know, having been stationed in the Thebaid so long, makes them dread your command to invade."

"Another Britannia? I'll have to send Narcissus to quell them." Claudius laughed and winked at Narcissus, who joined him in laughing.

"Of course, my emperor, your might can be exercised everywhere," I said. "But this is not Britannia, next to our prosperous province of Gallia, with our many legions stationed next door in Germania. The Thebaid, as you can imagine, is a desert inferno, removed from all civilization since it is so far from Alexandria. Divus Augustus was wise not to extend the empire into Ethiopia. The traders tell me that the gold stories are overdone and in fact you own the most important gold mine, as I've said, within our Egypt. Ivory, leather, and aromatics are the other goods our traders seek and it is a question whether such an invasion would be worthwhile. In my opinion, conquest of Parthia would be much more profitable."

To my surprise, Narcissus nodded in agreement. Perhaps the cost of supplying our 5th legion in the Thebaid and, temporarily the 10th, where everything had to be brought in from a distance and food rotted in a few days, made Narcissus hesitate. I was grateful for his support.

The emperor coughed and spit again into the piss pot. "So what do we need you for then?" he asked with a frown.

"To settle accounts with the fellaheen raped by our soldiers," I joked, anxious to get over the rough spot in the conversation.

"And how do you do that?" asked Narcissus.

"A denarius to the father. We have a slush fund. A denarius is more real money than they'll ever see in a lifetime."

"A denarius!" Claudius roared in amusement. "For a rape! To the father! I wish I'd get off so cheap with my women."

Narcissus and I joined in the laughter. Inside myself, I praised Yahweh, if there was a Yahweh, for the release of the tension.

Narcissus then spoke. "Let's go to the reason for this meeting. As you know, Tiberius, you don't need to stay in Rome. The emperor has decided that you should return to your post as epistrategus in the Thebaid. We know you are a loyal servant of the state and highly born. We will look for another post equal to your abilities. But nothing is available now."

I had difficulty swallowing my dismay. However, it was apparent, for Claudius said kindly, "We'll find something for you, Tiberius. But there is nothing at present. Be patient. And if things get too boring, try raping some fellaheen girls. One denarius! I ought to try myself."

With a friendly smile he gestured to the door. Narcissus got up. I gave the royal salute, bent to the waist, and left. Narcissus went with me to the outer door. "Don't worry," he said, "we'll find something for such a patriot," and went back inside.

I returned to the Thebaid, to the most boring two years of my life. My work by now was automatic and indeed I left most of it to my assistant while I diced and drank with the centurions of the 5th and 10th legions, who were equally bored. Once every two months I traveled up to Alexandria for a week. My parents were still alive but left word with an associate they had no desire to see me and that I was dead in their eyes. The Jews avoided me as an apostate. The Greeks were friendly in a formal way but knew my Jewish origins. Only the Great Library staff, where I spent part of my time, welcomed me as a high official of the state. Then there was the Hippodrome and of course the brothels. One week every two months and then back to the inferno. I started to drink too much and put on weight—eating and drinking were still a pleasure. And I was sliding toward middle age, a failure in my own eyes.

Shortly after my return to Egypt, I received official word that the invasion of Ethiopia was postponed by decision of the emperor, though probably that of Narcissus.

The 10th legion was soon sent back north to its base near Alexandria, which left me even fewer friends to drink with. The local whores here were ugly. Sometimes, when the heat was excessive for brief moments, I even envied my dead brother Marcus, now beyond worldly concerns. Time dragged on. I started to age.

In my third year in the Thebaid Emperor Claudius appointed me procurator of Judaea, the provincial governor in charge of military and civilian duties, a rather mysterious choice because by then he should have known through his mother that I was born a Jew. I think what determined his choice was the premature death of King

Agrippa I, at which time Claudius changed the status of Judaea from a self-governing client state to a Roman province; and he needed someone in whom he had complete faith. Besides, it may have seemed obvious to the emperor, if I were of Jewish origin, that my knowledge of the Judean religion would prove useful when dealing with such a restless and rebellious people. And in all circumstances as procurator I was under and responsible to the praefectus of Syria at Antiochia.

Emperor Claudius was right. By that I considered myself neither Jew nor Egyptian but rather a high official dedicated to the interests of the glorious Roman Empire, which had brought peace and prosperity to the greater part of the world—running from Britannia in the north to Mauretania in the south, and from Hispania in the west to Lesser Armenia in the east. What were the lives of a few thousand malcontents compared to the new roads constantly being built to tie the empire together, with new settlements developing resources and extending commerce, as well as converting barbarian peoples to civilization? Besides, anyone with sense knows the weak go down and the strong go up.

I was aware of course—putting aside the excesses of the four years of Emperor Caligula—that Augustus, Tiberius, and Claudius had what we raised of Jewish faith would call disgusting personal morals, yet those emperors were reasonably competent administrators, or appointed such men, under whom the empire flourished. Indeed, I got to know Emperor Claudius quite well after several visits on Egyptian business. Contrary to petty gossip, though he stammered, slobbered, and his body jerked oddly, he had an excellent mind. I read his studies of Etruscan history and society, I think the first on the subject, and they showed real scholarship. Of course his choice of wives was a disaster, but that was another story.

The post Emperor Claudius appointed me to as procurator of Judaea was a difficult one. I was there only two years and that was too long. I was not alone in this short posting because procurators were changed frequently under Claudius unlike under Tiberius.

The first thing I did as procurator was to hire a language teacher to learn Aramaic, the *lingua franca* of a good part of the Near East, including Judaea. Apparently Hebrew, their original language, was used mainly for ceremonial purposes though sometimes still spoken in Jerusalem. I had trouble learning to read the letters from right to left, unlike other civilized people. The letter shapes were also different, called Semitic. It took me all the two years I was there to speak and read with some skill the language of Aramaic.

My initial diplomatic call after arriving was to see the high priest, named Joseph, son of Qambit, who amusingly was related through marriage to my father. The Jews like most other peoples intermarry on the highest level, thus keeping the wealth and power in a relatively few families.

The high priest was cold, as could be expected toward a person considered an apostate and, following their custom, he kept seven paces away from me as though I were a leper. He told me there was agitation in Judaea, which was divided into three main sects. They were, firstly, the Sadducees, composed of the priestly caste and the rich aristocratic families. This group rejected any concept of future punishment or reward after death, belief in angels and spirits, and espoused free will. For the Sadducees, like for my Uncle Philo, only the Torah of Moses had divinity, not the oral law. The second group was the Pharisees, who believed, to the contrary, there was reward or punishment after death, were indecisive as to free will, and considered sacred the oral law as well as the Mosaic Torah. Understandably, their views were more popular with the common peoples who, rigidly nationalistic, thought of themselves as the heirs of the Maccabees, the earlier Judeans who had thrown off the yoke of the Greeks. And the third group was the Essenes, rather small in numbers, ascetic fanatics who lived frugally, despised money, studied the scriptures all the time, and rejected slavery.

Joseph, son of Qambit, added that there was a new small group who believed the long-awaited Messiah had come to save not only the Judeans but all mankind. They were called Yeshuites after their leader, Yeshua. However, they were considered rather a nuisance and their disciples mainly preached outside of Judaea. I remembered meeting them with my Uncle Philo at Alexandria when I was young, as well as hearing of them in Rome later.

Then the high priest said there were also two terrorist groups, one called the Zealots and the other called the Sicarii, or Dagger Men, who were professional assassins, killing or attempting to kill those Jews who were in favor of working with the Roman authorities. Thus Joseph, son of Qambit, said, in a sense it was as much a civil war as a patriotic revolution, the top level of society wanting to work with the Romans and the poorer people being in favor of a revolt come what may.

The real problem, he continued, was that Herod the Idumanean, grandfather of the recently deceased King Agrippa I, was a horrible human being but a great builder, not only of the Holy Temple in Jerusalem but many other buildings and desert fortresses such as Masada and Herodium. Though hated, his building projects kept the people employed and were good for business, with little time to organize revolts; as an example, 18,000 workers alone were employed on the temple. Emperor Augustus, who knew well his client kings, had a good sense of humor. Familiar with Jewish customs, on learning that Herod had killed so many of his sons, he was reported to have said, "I'd rather be Herod's pig than his son."

Now it was different, Joseph, son of Qambit, continued. At least with Herod, no matter how wasteful and how high the taxes most of the money stayed in Judaea, whereas with the Roman procurators they stole what they could and sent it to Rome instead. Unemployment was very high, and from the unemployed were recruited the radicals. Thus, Judaea was a country divided into factions, a kind of festering series of internal wars, the Sadducees against the Pharisees, the rich merchants against the poor peasants and the unemployed, and the radical groups who only agreed on killing Jews opposed to their aims. The sole unity of all these groups was the belief that the Judeans were the Chosen People of Yahweh and thus superior to all other peoples. Thus, the high priest concluded with a sigh, he could see no peace in sight.

On the issues of unemployment and taxation I soon learned that the high priest was right. The farmers, the overwhelming majority of the population, paid tremendous taxes: a third part of their produce, a quarter part of their fruit, and half of the wine and oil. Then there was the yearly tax for the Temple, the salt tax, and dues for the upkeep of roads and bridges. In my heart I knew the rebels had cause but all that existed before I became procurator and my job was to maintain order and not to promote or allow rebellion. Economics was surely a factor, as it was wherever the Romans taxed heavily and procurators sucked money with indifference to the plight of conquered people. But it was more than that here in Judaea, as I have noted. It can be summarized by a quote from one of their rabbis that was told to me: "With you alone [the Judeans] I have joined my name; I am not the Yahweh of the idolaters, but the Yahweh of Israel alone." That, the belief of the Chosen People, is what led to their fanaticism.

To make matters worse for me as procurator was that a long drought started in my first year and disorder increased. I was forced to double the night patrols, though cautioning the centurions to instruct the legionnaires to steer clear of the Temple precinct. Fortunately, a tributary state of Parthia, Adiabene, originally Assyria, was ruled by a queen who converted to Judaism, Helena by name, and she brought grain and figs to the famished country. I also may add that the political and religious tensions led to local revolts and I was forced to crucify two Judeans from the Galilee, Jacob and Shimon, sons of Judas, the founder of the Zealots, as well as hundreds of their inflamed followers. It was a very disagreeable post. I had no interest in milking the people but they hated me, thinking I would be like other procurators. Joseph, son of Qambit, revealed to the rabbis that I was an apostate, their reason to doubly hate me. The result was that I could not walk the streets without a large guard nor could I visit any of the holy sites. There were no brothels to comfort me since prostitution among the Jews was forbidden, a prohibition rigorously enforced by their religious leaders.

My sole consolation was that I made up with Princess Berenice, former widow of my brother Marcus, whose speckled career I will shortly touch on. A religious Jew, like our family a Roman aristocrat through grant by Julius Caesar to Herod the Great, her great-grandfather, she often left her brother's small kingdom in the north at Chalcis to stay at the Herodian property in Jerusalem. She too had made peace with the Romans and we sat around every night, now equals, talking of old times. If she weren't constantly involved with different men I might have had some thoughts on that line, for she was very beautiful. But it was better not to.

One religious fact I learned to my amusement was that my Uncle Philo, the most revered philosopher in Alexandria by both Greeks and Jews, was not highly regarded in Judaea. The reason was simple. Philo saw all truth to be in the Pentateuch, regarding the later oral law as irrelevant, or perhaps better said, of little importance. In Judaea on the other hand the rabbis who expanded and enlarged scriptural content were regarded as holy men, Yahweh's representatives. Thus, while my uncle denigrated or disregarded the rabbinic traditions, for the Pharisees they became more and more important, and hence my uncle's views less important. Philo's Hellenized Judaic allegories were also anathema to many Judeans. The ironic part was that the only group still taking my Uncle Philo's writing as fundamental to religious understanding was the Yeshuites, the dissident Jews who considered Yeshua as Cristos, the Messiah, that same group my uncle had mocked when taking me to their services in Alexandria while I was still an adolescent.

XV

At this point I, Professor David Fremont, found the scroll torn, with a section missing and both parts with tattered ends, the first part I had read as well as the second, probably due to mouse gnawing. I pulled together the edges of the two sections but it was apparent a part had been lost.

Then I was startled by a shake on my shoulder. Father Hieronymos was leaning over me. "It has been five hours since you've been sitting here as though in a trance. It is seven o'clock. Come to the refectory and at least take some soup. The brothers raise our own vegetables, as you know from the past, and we would be pleased to have you as our guest." He added with a chuckle, "Like old times. Maybe at last we can convert you to the true faith."

I smiled affectionately at Father Hieronymos. He was such a simple good man, a true Christian in the sense of Christ's teachings, not one of those bureaucrats who ran many churches.

"Done," I said and looked down at the scroll sections lying on the long table. "Don't leave," I warned them. "I haven't finished."

Father Hieronymos laughed and we walked to the refectory, where I was greeted with many an affectionate gaze from the monks who had known me for decades while I labored each summer cataloging the library manuscripts.

Grace said with heads dipped, the monks made the sign of the cross and we sat down to eat the delicious homemade pottage. There was little conversation. A spiritual bond held these ascetic brothers together. I had felt it for years and part of me envied them. "What a grace is true belief," I thought to myself—but I was incapable of reaching that spiritual height. Simple men as they were, with all my education, with two doctorates and command of seven languages, in a sense they were wiser than I.

"Back to work," I said to myself, shrugging off such thoughts. "Melancholia is a curse driven away by hard work." And rising from my chair, I thanked Father Hieronymos, nodded to the brothers, and returned to the library.

"See, the scroll sections are still there," Father Hieronymos, who had followed me, said with a faint touch of malice. "They did not flee to protect themselves from an unbeliever."

"*Ad astra per aspera*," I said, knowing Father Hieronymos understood Latin. "I will overcome."

"Speak Greek here," said the brother with a gentle frown.

"I would," I answered, "but I can't think of the Greek equivalent." And I sat down at the long table and pulled toward me the fractured edge of the second scroll section. I would of course never know what part of Tiberius Julius Alexander's life I missed in the lost piece.

XVI

As *procurator provinciae*, imperial administrator in the important province of Syria for over a decade, life was far more interesting though of course I had to ingratiate myself with Lucius Valerius Marsus, the highborn praefectus over me. Annexed by the great General Pompey a century before, Syria was thoroughly Romanized. Life at Antiochia, the capital city, was very pleasant, unlike my two miserable years in Jerusalem.

Antiochia was the third city in size in the empire. It was situated on a fertile plain at the Orontes River close to the Great Sea, through which wares were shipped to Greece and Rome. It was a main trade center for the goods from the Euphrates River, Judaea, and even Egypt. As a great Roman metropolis there were theatres, baths, and a circus. Noted for its lax morals, Antiochia had fine brothels as well as similar places for those with different sexual tastes.

One of my duties, partly relating to the lax morals, was acting as umpire in the constant conflict between Jews and Greeks, the former holding fast to their strict moral beliefs while the Greeks were far more relaxed and skeptic. There was constant brawling between the two groups. Emperor worship was also part of this problem. The Greeks had no difficulty to include the emperors as divinities in their litany of gods while the Jews would die before profaning their Yahweh. A favorite game of the Greeks was to place at night in Jewish centers carved statues of the emperor as a divine being. A constant belief of Jew-haters, written by some Egyptian historian, was that the Jews worshiped an ass's head which was kept in their Holy of Holies in Jerusalem. The Greeks would sneak into Jewish temples and put on their altars the severed head of an ass. The Jews, who were better street fighters, perhaps because of their blind religious faith, would then attack the Greeks and break skulls. The Greeks would complain to Lucius Valerius Marsus, who in disgust over the bickering would turn the matter over to me. The Greeks offered money; the Jews likewise. I would refuse to take their bribes and try to act with impartial justice, which infuriated both parties.

My real job was different and far more important. Because of the high nobility of our praefectus, Emperor Claudius, always suspicious of disloyalty, came to depend on me in the negotiations involving relations with our Eastern client states in the constant tension with the powerful Partian enemy. Narcissus, whose original distrust of me had changed, likewise encouraged the emperor to depend on me. Inevitably this caused friction with Lucius Valerius Marsus but by my studied humbling before him this did not lead to an open break.

My important work may best be explained by a long talk I had with Narcissus, who called me to Rome early in my appointment.

After entering the door of the imperial palace I was met by him alone and without the usual guards, showing his continued trust in me. Instead of going to the main door where the emperor met his guests, Narcissus gestured toward another door, to the left, and went in before me.

The large room was magnificently paneled in fine-grained dark wood, I think mahogany. Along parallel walls were set seats of the same wood, on which rested white silk cushions. In the center of the room was a long table, of matching wood, with marble insets on the sides showing nymphs chased by satyrs. Set against the table were two chairs side by side. On the table lay a large parchment map titled at the top *The Eastern Provinces and Adjacent Territories*.

Narcissus sat down on one chair and beckoned me to sit on the other. "By the way I believe this is our fifth meeting," he said. "I want to ask you now that we're alone together how come a Julio-Claudian named Tiberius Julius has the last name Alexander. You know I'm Greek and felt warm toward you soon enough as a Greek with such a name. And I've heard you speak Greek fluently, as of course I do, as well as Latin, still a bit difficult for me."

"To answer the second part of your question is easy," I said. "We spoke Greek at home, the language of all civilized Alexandrians. And the good Latin is due to my being sent from childhood to the best academy in that city where both Greek and Latin were spoken and taught together.

"As to my name Alexander, of which I too am proud of, it is a bit of a mystery. The royal name of Julius was given to my father by Divus Augustus and probably the family received the name Alexander from one of the Greek Ptolemy rulers for similar services rendered."

Narcissus smiled. "As a Greek also proud of being a Roman, we thus both share the honor. Now let's get to work." He gestured to the large map on the table and took out a stylus, pointing as he talked.

"As you undoubtedly know, the Euphrates River is the boundary between us and the Parthian Empire, our great enemy. To the east of the boundary, their side, lies the region of Mesopotamia, including Babylonia to the south, between the Euphrates and Tigris rivers, a very fertile area. To the east of the Tigris River lies Assyria, and then Media, those being the important regions of the Parthian Empire.

"On our side of the Euphrates border," Narcissus continued, again pointing with the stylus, "to the south is the province of Judaea, which includes Galilee, both turbulent areas. Carved out of the northeastern Galilee is the small state of Chalcis, held by King Agrippa II, a tried and true dependent of Rome. North stretches our great province of Syria, where of course you serve, flanked to the east by our vassal states of Cappadocia and Lesser Armenia. The large independent kingdoms of Greater Armenia and Georgia to the north of Parthia are grab bags for us or Parthia, falling to one or the other at different times.

"A wonderful overall picture," I said. "But why call me to Rome to discuss this? Do you want me to get involved in an invasion of Greater Armenia?" I asked with excitement.

As though taking a completely different tack in the conversation, Narcissus put down the stylus and sat back, his open mouth showing large yellow teeth. "Are you aware," he asked, "of the continued friction at Rome between our high military and our civil administrations, the latter of which I head?"

"You mean the problem with General Gnaeus Domitius Corbulo?" I asked.

"That's the best example. Corbulo, indeed a very capable general, wants to be a new Julius Caesar. You may have heard that as both praefectus and commanding general in Germania Superior he marched across our frontier on the Rhine, conquered the Frisians, and compelled them to swear allegiance to Rome.

"Good! But then, without orders from Rome, Corbulo then decided to march farther and enlarge the empire. Without orders! Claudius commanded him to pull back, which he reluctantly did, speaking unkind words about our emperor, as my spies reported."

"What was the problem?" I asked. "What's wrong with enlarging our glorious empire?"

Narcissus almost snarled. "My dear Tiberius, you sound like General Corbulo. What's the problem? The problem is economics, which no general—unlike our administrative staff—ever thinks about. Do you know that we have a half million legionnaires as a standing army? They need to be fed and clothed and housed and armed. In twenty years they retire and get a pension. And the praetorian guards get double pay."

"But you supported me when I suggested at one meeting with the emperor that we conquer Parthia."

"Yes, and absorb Mesopotamia, a breadbasket, the most fertile soil after Egypt in the world. Do you also remember I agreed with you about not attacking Ethiopia, where our legionnaires would die from the tsetse flies, as you said and which I confirmed. And also, which I likewise checked, the gold mines there are not very important. So we didn't make that error.

"But what have the forests of eastern Germania to offer? Nothing! Except the cost of legions to keep tranquil the region against those wild barbarians worth nothing of value for us to fight for except surly slaves."

Narcissus wrapped the large map with a hairy hand and gritted his yellow teeth. "Conquer what is profitable and can be held. Yes, conquer fertile land, not jungle or forest, conquer countries with rich mines and not sandy waste. This is what I am saying. And I have convinced our emperor after the cost of taking Britannia and crushing the revolt in Mauretania. Be powerful, all powerful, but be prudent, advice which actually follows the policy of Divus Augustus, who fixed the boundaries for Germania at the Danube and Rhine rivers, and refused to hold Ethiopia."

I sat back. I didn't speak for a minute. Nor did Narcissus. Finally I said, "I think your analysis is amazing. I always gloried in the triumphs of our generals, including Corbulo, whom I have admired. But I now see what you say makes sense. In fact it comes to mind, aside from his early death, that was the weakness of our beloved Alexander the Great, extending the lines too far too soon so his empire fell apart after his death. But how do I fit into your marvelous analysis? I never appoint the generals nor control the monies."

Narcissus looked at me intently. "Subversion."

"What?!"

"You heard me. Subversion. Are you aware that more free cities, and even countries, have been won or lost by smart bribery than by marching legions? It was even a factor in our deadly struggle with Carthage, when we convinced Hannibal's African allies to desert him before the final assault."

"I didn't know that," I said. "But who am I to subvert or bribe?"

"This conversation is very private, not even to be shared with

Lucius Valerius Marsus, your praefectus, who already is suspicious of your intimacy with our emperor and thinks you spy on him for us."

"Do you want me to, like in Britannia?"

"No, frankly we have others do that."

"And on me as well," I quipped.

Narcissus laughed. "Perhaps. But all reports indicate you are completely loyal. You are a true supporter of our emperor."

I nodded vigorously. Narcissus continued.

"The client states of Cappodocia and Lesser Armenia are weak allies. If they felt Parthia would be a winner in that region they would desert us. But they are a lesser problem because Parthia is poorer than we are and can't subsidize to the same extent. And it costs us less to buy their kings and tribal leaders than to maintain several legions permanently stationed there. In others words, exploit the national and regional rivalries by diplomacy and bribery to divide, maintain supremacy, and keep their states from the control of Parthia.

"The real problem is Greater Armenia. It is next to Parthia and a great distance from our two legions in Syria and our backup legion in Judaea."

"Why then bother?" I asked. "As far as I know, the Armenians don't have rich mines or very fertile soil. Why should we care?"

"Here it is a matter of geography, if I may put it that way," said Narcissus, leaning back in his chair. "The Parthians, like us, are aggressive and fine fighters. As we look with hungry eyes on Mesopotamia, so they do at our Syria, which once indeed belonged to their predecessors, the Persians. They also have ambitious generals who think of glory and can never forget the humiliating defeat by Alexander the Great over Persia. In the time of Divus Augustus they indeed captured one of our legion eagles, one of the only four we ever lost, the other three being of course in Germania."

"And what shall I do?" I asked.

"Wait for orders. You will, as at the invasion of Britannia, receive them in a code you alone will know, plus large sums of money. And above all be careful in dealing with Lucius Valerius Marsus, your praefectus, who would love to charge you with treason. The money will come from another source, through our Judean procurator Felix, a relation by marriage to the emperor and a man we also trust."

I have dictated to my educated Greek slave Isocrates the memory of that conversation with some care because it was a high step in my career, which eventually brought me to the top of the Roman military world. In effect I was given the authority, subject to general orders, to control our relations with Parthia, our sole great enemy with a large empire and one equally aggressive.

To understand my subversive activities, whose one policy was to weaken Parthia, it is necessary to give a brief review of that empire's situation.

King Gotarzes had become ruler of Parthia two years before I was sent to Syria. When former King Artabenus died over a decade before, he was succeeded by his son Vardanus, but the next year Gotarzes, also of the royal family, revolted. The civil war resulted in a defeat of Gotarzes, who fled. Then King Vardanus was killed in a palace intrigue organized by his rival three years later and Gotarzes became king.

Narcissus was unhappy with King Gotarzes, an aggressive ruler, and my job had been to subsidize not only our vassal kings in Lesser Armenia and Cappadocia to stay neutral in the Parthian civil war but also to support Vardanus. We also had at Rome as a hostage in this confusing period a Parthian prince, Mehefdates, and we released him and subsidized his army as a candidate to fight Gotarzes, who, however, defeated him. As a result I wrote Narcissus to instruct Lucius Valerius Marsus, our Syrian praefectus—I was still an underground agent—to warn King Gotarzes that if he invaded Greater Armenia it would mean war with Rome. Fortunately for us Gortazes was assassinated in turn shortly thereafter. I would like to take credit for this happy event, which so pleased Emperor Claudius, yet it was not my doing but rather another of their typical internal revolts among those Oriental despots.

Oddly, my job of sowing dissent was made easier by the kinship among the heads of the Eastern states, which often led to these family murders. Another good example is that of King Mithridates III, who also ruled in this period. He came to power in Media, the eastern area of Parthia, by murdering his father with the help of Orodes, his brother. The two brothers then warred. Mithridates lost, fled, and appealed to us for help. We advanced him funds to raise a new army but he was again beaten and killed, his brother then assuming the title of Orodes I.

It was an exciting job and I got to know quite well the different rulers and their states, indeed better than did Lucius Valerius Marsus, our Syrian praefectus and technically my superior. As a result Emperor Claudius through Narcissus became more and more dependent on my advice. This naturally angered Marsus. In fact Narcissus sent me an amusing scroll through Felix, procurator of Judaea, in which Marsus, correctly noting my frequent trips to our vassal states, accused me of treason, of conspiring with Parthia. Narcissus had a clever answer. He stated that my trips were authorized by the emperor because, having spent two years as procurator of Judaea, I was the sole person in the eastern administration who knew Aramaic, the *lingua franca* of the entire area, and therefore indispensable when dealing with kings and tribal leaders. I laughed when I thought of the chagrin of Marsus.

The years flew by. It was status quo with Parthia, acceptable to Emperor Claudius. Then everything changed when he married Agrippina, his own niece, who soon dominated him. Finally she succeeded in getting the emperor to reject his own son Britannicus as the legitimate heir, replacing him with Nero, her son by a former marriage. Then, through the aid of his food taster, Agrippina murdered Claudius with a dish of poisoned mushrooms. Following this she had Britannicus killed as well as Narcissus, who had supported Britannicus as the legitimate heir. All this occurred five years after I had been shifted to Syria.

At first, despite the murder of Narcissus, little changed for me. The administrative corps in Rome remained and my duties were the same. But in a short time Emperor Nero, leaving adolescence, showed his true colors. Gaius Ofonius Tigellinus, a sinister Sicilian, became the tool for orgies and crimes in which the emperor indulged. An alleged conspiracy led to the liquidation of nineteen of the highest noblemen. Generals were killed as well, including the commanders of both Germania Superior and Germania Inferior.

Rome weakened from these purges while Parthia grew stronger. Vologasus, a new and great king now coming to the throne there, took advantage of the tumult and conquered Greater Armenia, setting his brother Tiridates on that throne. The threat to our vassal states and even Syria itself was obvious. General Corbulo, our greatest living general, who had somehow escaped Nero's bloodbaths, was sent to Syria to redeem the situation.

There had probably not been such a brilliant Roman commander since Agrippa and Germanicus, the mainstays of Divus Augustus. General Gnaeus Domitius Corbulo, commanding general of Germania Superior under Claudius, as noted, had pushed back the Germans to the Rhine and was paused to strike further against orders when the emperor ordered him to withdraw, which he sullenly did. In disgrace for acting without instructions, he had been passed over until the Parthian crisis brought him to the fore again.

Corbulo was a formidable figure. Born at Placentia, northern Liguria, he spoke with a local Latin dialect. Tall, fair skinned, with thick blond hair and sharp blue eyes, Corbulo must have come from German stock, which in an earlier age moved south into Italy. His very appearance scared most people and I was too at first. However, we soon became friends or as friendly as one could be with such a cold figure. The reason, as I soon discovered, was that he respected my intricate knowledge of our Roman vassal states, their roads, their cities, their fortifications, and their borders with each other and with Parthia, all essential information for him. And when he found out that I had been responsible for building the highway through the desert on our side of the Euphrates River, which connected to Antiochia, and so knew intimately the western border of Parthia, this led him to look on me as an important colleague. In fact, in his second year in Syria he raised me to his *minister bello*, his war minister. The disgusted Syrian praefectus Marsus must have been glad to get rid of me.

The two Syrian legions defeated by the Parthians were in disorder. A stern taskmaster, the first thing General Corbulo set out to do—and it took two years—was to reestablish rigid discipline. His initial move was to bring to Syria the famous legion Legio XV Apollinarius, which served so well under him on the Rhine. Calling together their centurions with the centurions of the two Syrian legions, he pointed out the difference in the latter's sloppy clothing, their parading half-naked, often drunk by midday, their unshaven faces, and general disorder. He stated that the Syrian centurions, like the common soldiers, would be scourged if they did not shortly rise up in discipline to those of the Legio XV. Army soldiers henceforth, including centurions, he emphasized, would be flogged and docked in pay, with no wine rations, if not properly shaven, dressed, and carrying full military equipment at all times.

At first the soldiers of the two Syrian legions, stationed for years at licentious Antiochia, did not take the matter seriously. They soon woke up to the new reality under General Corbulo when not only legionnaires but centurions were flogged and even one soldier was crucified for having a Parthian mistress, which Corbulo considered treason. But the conduct of the Legio XV impressed them most when Corbulo instructed the centurions of that legion to remove the protective buttons from their sword and spear tips while dueling in practice with lazy soldiers; several as a result were stabbed in the belly and chest, sometimes fatally. With such iron discipline, in two years the Syrian legions were on a par with those of Legio XV. The new rules were hard indeed, but effective.

General Corbulo was now ready. Without orders from Rome he struck at Greater Armenia and captured the important city of Artaxata, the Armenian northern capital, located at the end of the Euphrates River where that state and Parthia met to the northeast. He stopped at the border.

The Parthian army was no match for the revitalized Roman troops. King Vologasus sued for peace. Then General Corbulo made the mistake similar to that he committed in Germania. Rather than clearing with Rome, perhaps swollen in prestige, he unilaterally signed a peace treaty with the Parthian king that the two empires would both evacuate Greater Armenia.

Emperor Nero was enraged at that breach of discipline and ordered Corbulo to leave Syria, which he did. Nero then sent another general to invade Greater Armenia, who was soundly defeated. Nero, swallowing his pride, ordered Corbulo back to Syria to avoid a Parthian invasion. The brilliant Corbulo, again given supreme command, in no time smashed his way through Greater Armenia up to Parthia, routing the enemy. King Tiridates of Greater Armenia, though a brother to the Parthian king, accepted the inevitable and stated he would retake his position as that country's ruler, however, as a subject to Rome. I, as *minister bello* under Corbulo, together with Vivianus Annius, Corbulo's son-in-law, accompanied Tiridates to Rome, where he knelt on his knees before Nero as a sign of abject defeat. King Vologasus of Parthia, a realist, also signed the accord.

Actually, the initial plan of attack had been a coordinated pincer movement. General Corbulo would strike as he did, but instead of stopping at the Greater Armenia border with Parthia he would push south down the Tigris River in Parthia while I would lead troops along the highway I had built from Antiochia to the Euphrates River and cross the river at the point I knew least fortified. Then we would meet and cut Parthia in half, hopefully trapping King Vologasus.

The plan had been reluctantly given up by Corbulo when, knowing best the areas involved, I had pointed out, with the support of the general staff, that his plan was not only in defiance of Emperor Nero's order to avoid invading Parthia but also that our lines of communication and supplies would have to pass through many hundreds of miles of enemy territory, some of it desert, while King Vologasus could retreat into eastern Media, his homeland, and wait patiently until we were exhausted. General Corbulo, who imagined himself as a new Julius Caesar, finally agreed to limit our invasion to the conquest of Greater Armenia.

Nero's ego was satisfied by the abject submission of King Tiridates but not his vengeance at the defiance by Corbulo when he negotiated unilaterally. Now that peace was established there was no longer need for the brilliant general, whom the emperor increasingly distrusted. He had also watched with fear the Roman people's idolatry of Corbulo. Undoubtedly influenced by Tigellinus, his hated minister, the two together concocted a plan to eliminate the general. It was simple but clever.

Nero at this time was going to Corinth in Greece to dedicate the digging of a canal. He sent a note to Corbulo congratulating him on his achievement and told the general to meet him there. Corbulo, separated from his admiring generals and centurions, sailed to the port of Athens only accompanied by his son-in-law. He was met there by a short scroll personally signed by Nero directing him to commit suicide, which he did.

In Antiochia we were stunned by the news. That the most beloved of all Roman military leaders of our time obeyed so quickly—because with the hatred for Nero he could probably have seized the empire—was strange but not unique in a man whose whole career was based on military discipline. And he told his son-in-law "I deserved it" before stabbing himself in the throat. The only possible reason is that he realized he had been wrong to disobey imperial orders two times.

XVII

The suicide of General Corbulo did not affect my career negatively. On the contrary, for with the Parthian danger no longer a problem (the joint treaty of nonaggression was signed and held up for many years), peace reigned throughout the empire except for the usual German disturbances.

Over the decades of my career in the military and civil administrations I had made high friends in Rome. I was no threat to Nero for, though of the Julio-Claudian line by adoption, I was not by gens. It was suggested by these friends, and Nero agreed, to advance me to the very high post of *praefectus Alexandrae et Aegptus*, or governor of all Egypt. My background as a former epistrategus of the Thebaid in southern Egypt, my knowledge of the language, the customs, as well as the administrative workings, were without question determining factors.

This was one of the great posts of Rome since the control of the grain deliveries to the capital was vital. And I, an Egyptian Jew by birth! None of my immediate family except my mother lived to see this brilliant elevation but it was just as well. For it was when returning in triumph to Alexandria I had learned of the death of my father. On a commercial trip to Parthia right before we with General Corbulo were crossing into Greater Armenia, threatening the Parthian capital, King Vologasus of that country had imprisoned all foreigners of Roman and Greek origin; and my father had been treated very roughly, Gaius Julius being an aristocratic Roman name and Alexander being the name of the conqueror whom all Parthians, successors to the Persians, despised. I was told by another hostage my father simply didn't wake up one morning.

I was informed as well that our family fortune had been much reduced after a century of prominence, which meant little to me since my parents were the sole survivors, excepting my mother now being the only one alive, and I was very well paid in my high state positions. I was likewise told that my father never again mentioned my name and that after our fight many years ago he had sat in prayer for the prescribed Jewish seven days of mourning following the death of a family member.

Out of respect and pity the congregation at the Alexandrian *proseuche* had continued to call up my father for the first of the triennial cycle of the reading of the Torah, and let him retain his chair next to the seat of Moses; but I was also told that no one had ever seen him smile again. And with the death of my two uncles Philo and Lysimachos, and that of my brother Marcus, plus the fact that I never married and had no children, the Julio-Claudian family of Alexandria would die with me.

Since I had been so honored by the appointment as governor of Egypt by Nero, I might add a note comparing him with Caligula, the two most hated Roman emperors. Both started their reigns in mild and commendable manners. Both turned out to be monsters with no regard for anything but their own personal and strange pleasures. But there were differences, aside from the fact that Caligula was emperor for somewhat less than four years while Nero reigned for fourteen years.

Caligula, with whom I fortunately had little to do, was most likely insane from an excessive love potion given him by his wife Caesonia, for he displayed obvious signs of mental illness. He was only twenty-nine when killed but according to my associates at Rome he had many early marks of abnormality: inability to sleep more than a few hours at night, nightmares, hallucinations, mental wanderings, and erratic behavior. He was very tall, pale, with a heavy body but slender neck, and his eyes were shrunk in his head. He also had the falling sickness, fainting without reason. He was alert enough, however, as I believe I mentioned, at the start of his reign among his butcheries to kill Gemellus, grandson of Tiberius and a legitimate heir to the throne.

The basis for this strange behavior was the belief he was truly a living god, similar to Alexander the Great. As an example, he chopped off the heads of the marble statues from or in Graecia, including those of Jupiter Olympicus, and substituted his own head. He ordained a special temple to himself as divine, with priests and sacrifices, dominated by his statue in gold. To aggrandize his name, he insisted that it was the result of incest committed by Divus Augustus and his daughter Julia. He killed many members of the royal family without reason, accusing them falsely of treason. By a miracle his uncle Claudius, the future emperor, survived only because Caligula liked to poke fun at him as an imbecile, and thus he seemed no threat.

Besides incest with his own sister he took any woman he desired, married or single, common or noble, and then with relish would describe their sexual habits in detail. To get money for his ludicrous and wasteful practices and orgies he declared invalid the wills of rich men and seized their property.

Caligula reigned such a short time because his praefectorian guard was frightened by his sick boasts that he could have them all killed whenever he felt so inclined. In their joy at his murder, they stabbed him repeatedly in his genitals, killing as well his wife Caesonia and his daughters.

Emperor Nero, unlike Caligula, was not so much insane as rather a horrible sadist who took pleasure in murder, often designed to give great pain. I can recount two such practices as told to me. One was to invite a guest to dinner who he wanted to kill. He would ply the unsuspecting victim with large quantities of wine and then have the person's penis tied tightly so he could not pass urine. While the victim screamed in agony from blood poisoning, Nero would smile and often play the harp. Another sadistic act was that he would dress in the skin of a wild beast and bite the genitals of nude men tied to posts, often then ordering them killed. A grotesque activity also told to me was that he cut off the genitals of a handsome young man and then used him as a woman, which wits in Rome then whispered it was too bad his father hadn't done that.

Like Caligula, he killed without remorse. Coming to be emperor with dubious legitimacy because his adopted father, Emperor Claudius, as mentioned, had a real son named Britannicus by Messalina, an earlier wife, his later wife Agrippina schemed with success to have her son Nero be placed first in Claudius's will.

Nero arranged with his mother's aid to poison Britannicus. Whether insecure or simply a lover of cruelty, he murdered everyone close to the seat of power, including any possible heirs: besides his brother, his mother, his sister, his son-in-law, his stepson, the captain of the praetorian guard, and even the renowned philosopher Seneca, who had been his tutor when young. Angry at something his wife said, he kicked her in the stomach when she was in a late state of pregnancy, causing her death as well. It was related that when he sent men to kill his mother, whom he feared, she pulled up her dress exposing her stomach and said, "Stab here where I made this monster," although it was commonly felt she deserved her fate.

Nero likewise murdered many of the Roman senators still left, planning but being dissuaded to poison those remaining. A favorite line of his was "*lupus est homo homini*"—man is a wolf to his fellow man; and that every man would do what he Nero did if possessing absolute power, which of course was false, as Divus Augustus was the proof.

Oddly, for most of us who directed the empire in distant provinces or were high in the military, we not only had little to fear from Caligula or Nero but were encouraged to stay in office and even advanced in position—as was I—so long as there was no disturbance or lack of tribute money. Caligula and Nero were so obsessed with their own sick pleasures that in an odd way the empire prospered by their lack of interest. All their disgusting activities took place in a small top circle of imperial Rome. It was mainly when a military man of high noble birth such as Commander Corbulo became popular and thus a threat that Nero arranged his killing.

For those of us who were born in the provinces or were not of high Roman nobility, Emperor Nero was no threat at all. Furthermore, his disinterest in expanding the empire (he even considered giving up Britannia) brought peace and security to the soldiers of the legions. One might add ironically that Nero was also so successful in purging the Roman Julio-Claudian aristocracy that he put an end to it and thus opened the empire to what might be new meritorious leadership, as indeed Vespasian turned out to be.

My term as governor of Egypt started with a disaster personally affecting me. It was due to the same old problem, the tension and hatred between the Greeks and the Jews of Alexandria. The riots created in that city by Flaccus over a quarter century earlier had never calmed. They had been suppressed, which is very different. An incident, seemingly minor on the surface, occurred, which threw Alexandria into complete turmoil.

After I was appointed praefectus, King Agrippa II, from his small kingdom in northern Galilee created for him by the influence of his late father King Agrippa I of Judaea with Emperor Caligula, came to Alexandria to congratulate me. This was natural enough since his sister Princess Berenice had been married to my unfortunate dead brother Marcus and thus made us related by marriage. Agrippa II entertained lavishly in the Jewish community, and included a review of the voluntary militia which had been organized for self-defense after the Flaccus insurrection.

The Greeks saw this visit, and the review of the Jewish militia, as a threat or conspiracy since the Judean revolt in the Galilee had broken out the same year. They organized a general assembly at the amphitheatre to send an embassy to Emperor Nero assuring their loyalty. The underlying theme of course was to question the loyalty of the new governor, myself, who they knew had been born a Jew. Some Jews attended the meeting out of curiosity and, being recognized, were attacked as "enemies" and "spies." Most escaped but three were caught and burned alive.

The Jewish militia, on learning this, rose in fury and attempted to set fire to the amphitheatre with the Greeks inside. King Agrippa II hastily left Egypt but the tension had gone too far and both sides armed for a confrontation.

As governor I attempted to resolve the matter peacefully. I sent for the Jewish elders and leading citizens to plead for calm or I would have to call out the legions stationed in Egypt. But their leaders would or could not listen, and indeed a muffled voice from the back of the room ridiculed me as an apostate. I was thus forced to call in the two legions, instructing them to enter the Delta quarter, where almost all of the Jews lived and, as a severe lesson not only to kill the rioters but to sack their property.

The carnage only ended when I saw my severity was well learned. Thousands of Jews were killed—a later estimate of 50,000 was an exaggeration—and the property loss was tremendous. The Jewish community, between the previous Flaccus riots and the suppression of this later revolt, never regained its prosperity. But the lesson was learned; during the Judean War then occurring, Alexandrian Jewry was quiet. The Jews had been about one-third of the city's populace before; not only were they fewer now but also weaker economically. I had done a good job as the governor and received a personal message of congratulations from Emperor Nero. Truth to tell, I felt my obligation to keep peace as praefectus was more important than the lives of those fanatic Jews. I knew well their mentality, my father having been one of them—and often heard ringing in my ears his remark: "Better Tiberius than Marcus," after my brother had been killed. I suppose an astute Greek philosopher might read something in that tormenting thought and my action.

One result did penetrate the wall built around my origins. I heard the story from a faithful servant of our family. I was sitting in my office studying some official papers when one of my guards entered. I looked up, annoyed.

"Excuse me, sir," he said, "but an old Jew came here to talk to you. I told him to go to the Hades but he kept insisting, saying he worked for your family when you were a boy and had some important news for you."

"Ridiculous," I said, with a strange foreboding.

"That's what I thought," the guard said. "But he told me to tell you his name was Jeremiah and you would remember him."

I swallowed. Of course I remembered Jeremiah. He had worked for our family since I was a very young boy. My heart beat faster. "He may have some information on the recent riot. I'll give him a minute. Show him in."

The guard looked surprised but returned with Jeremiah after searching him. Bowing deeply, the old servant remained silent for a minute. Then here was his story.

It seems that all the family servants fled our mansion at the start of the riot except two who set themselves before the door to my mother's bedroom with knives from the kitchen. The legionnaires broke into our house, sacking all the gold, silver, and rare porcelain ware. Then they went up to the second floor where my mother cowered in her bed.

One of the two servants—Jeremiah, as it turns out—hid in a closet outside the bedroom. The other, a religious Jew who I also knew from childhood, had stood before the bedroom door with knife raised. Three legionnaires leaped at him with swords extended and stabbed him to death. Then they kicked down the door, went to the bed, pulled back the sheets under which my mother was hiding, and killed her as well.

"By the way," Jeremiah added as he bowed his head again in reverence before leaving, "I forgot to tell you something else that happened a long time ago, just after you left to go to Rome. I remember it because the girl was so beautiful. As you know," he continued, "we the servants in the family took turns guarding the main door. We couldn't have sentry dogs because your mother coughed so much when around dog hair."

"Anyhow," he said, "I was standing at the door one day when there was a knock. I looked through the peep hole and saw this girl standing outside. She was no threat, as was obvious, and I opened the door. She was really beautiful, with straw-blond hair and green eyes." He continued . . .

"Is Tiberius home?" she asked in a kind of trembling voice.

As you know the library is to the right of the entry door and your father happened to be working on some papers at the time. He heard an unknown female voice, and curious, came to the door.

"Good afternoon," the girl said though it was almost evening. "May I speak to Tiberius?" Her voice shook a bit. "Is he home?"

"And who are you?" your father asked. Unusual for him with a poorly dressed stranger, his voice was calm and polite.

"My name is Penelope," the girl said. "Is Tiberius home?" she repeated.

"No, he is not," your father said, eyeing the girl from tip to toe. His eyes then flickered to her stomach, which seemed a bit large for one so young.

"When will he be home?" she asked timidly.

Your father, as we all know, was one of the shrewdest men who ever lived. Whether he may have heard some gossip about you with a Greek girl, which was probable, his quick mind responded.

"Tiberius isn't home. Indeed he won't be home for two years. He graduated from the academy a month ago and wanted to continue his philosophical studies. Since he had done so well at school, I assented and we sent him to the most advanced collegium, the Plato Academy in Athens. He just left two weeks ago. At this point we don't even know his address in Athens."

"Two years!" the young girl said with a gasp.

"Two years," your father repeated. "Sorry."

I was standing behind your father. I saw tears come to the girl's eyes. She hesitated as though to say something, decided not to, said "Thank you, sir," and walked away. Curiously, I could have sworn I saw a look of pity on your father's face. He saw me watching him and commanded roughly, "Bring me a glass of red wine. Mareotis wine. I am going back to the library." It was so unusual for him to drink before dinner, before the blessing over the bread, I remembered that.

"Not of course that any of this means anything," the aged servant said. "But for some reason it just came to mind. Maybe it was because it was right before your unfortunate brother Marcus's wedding to the beautiful Princess Berenice. She was equally a beauty, that girl, though of lighter skin and northern looking, obviously Greek and not one of us."

I sat for a moment in silence. Then I took out two aureii and said, "Thank you. Buy something for yourself."

Such gold was a small fortune for Jeremiah. He bowed to the waist. "You have no idea how we who knew you as a boy are so proud of your great rise in the world. Your mother and father were blessed. Yahweh now grant your mother peace, as I am sure he has for your father."

Bowing his head again, he left. A simple and uneducated man, I was certain that Jeremiah had no idea that I was the one as praefectus of Egypt who had called out the legions that killed my mother.

After Jeremiah was gone I tore up and threw in the wastebasket the congratulatory message from Emperor Nero, changed into coarse working clothes, and went to a cheap tavern in the Beta quarter of Alexandria. Then I drank until I passed out. When I awoke, dragged from the tavern and dumped on the street after the tavern closed, I went to an all-night brothel-tavern and again, disdaining the whores, drank myself into another stupor. The blood that had poured from my mother's body at her death, I kept thinking, was the same blood in which I was born. The bed in which she was killed was the same bed in which, frightened as a child, I had cuddled up against her to my father's disapproval. Why had I not visited my mother since I became governor of all Egypt when my office was only a short distance away from the family mansion? Was it because of my being ashamed of my Jewish origin? And then I thought of Penelope and her attempt to visit me. And what did Jeremiah mean when he said that Penelope's stomach seemed enlarged?

It was early morning. Two Greeks stopped.

"He looks like he might be a Jew," one said.

"Impossible. This is the Beta quarter. They don't live here."

"He's got a kind of hooked nose and dark skin, but I agree he's so flushed with wine you can't tell."

"So do some of those damn Romans, particularly the nose." The second Greek leaned over me. "Zeus, what a stink. He's been drinking and vomiting. The bastard's pants are wet from piss."

"He's probably an Arab from the other side of the river celebrating something."

One of them gave me a kick that would have broken my ribs if it weren't for the workman's shirt. Then he spit on me and the two moved on.

I lay prostrate. My first thought again was of my mother bleeding to death because of my order for the legions to sack, pillage, and kill to teach the obstinate Jews a lesson. Then I thought of Penelope. Why had she come to see me after her abrupt rejection of my attempted overtures to reunite?

I had a sharp thought to kill myself. What was there about me that led to the deaths of all those close to me? My only moment of gratitude was that my Uncle Philo had passed away twelve years before and never knew of my actions. The words from the congratulatory scroll of Emperor Nero came back to mock me. *Macte virtute*, well done.

I groaned again and got up and staggered to my spacious headquarters, passing two legionnaire guards who eyed me with astonishment written wide across their faces.

XVIII

Every high Roman official in the outposts of the empire—and indeed some in Rome as well—has a special security force whose sole duty is to circulate among the population to report any subversive activity. I did too. Mine was made up of two separate groups, one Greek and one Jewish. I received weekly reports and relied on their accuracy.

Jeremiah's story of Penelope visiting my father's mansion brought her memory back to me in full force, though almost every week would go by with my thinking of her, usually in my dreams; and then asleep or awake I would close my mind to her memory. I had never married; I had made a decision, as I noted before, never to suffer the agony of such love again.

But of course by now Penelope would be middle-aged, surely married and probably with several children. The thought aroused my curiosity. I called in a young Greek man, Solon by name, one of my brightest agents and also obviously Macedonian by descent. I told him that in my youth I had studied at the top Alexandrian academy and often looked up reference material at the Great Library, being helped there by a learned librarian named Timoclea, Macedonian as was he. The librarian often met his daughter after work at the librarian entrance—women of course not being admitted—and once introduced her to me. I remembered her name was Penelope. A tax problem had come up regarding a family estate with the name of Timoclea and I wanted to check as to possible descendants.

Solon, my agent, went to work. A week later he came back with a report. I was correct. There had been a librarian at the Great Library with that name who, they told him, did have a daughter named Penelope—Solon praised my memory. But the librarian was dead and no one knew more.

I reminded Solon that in the annual city registration married women also had to register their maiden names and told him to look for the name Timoclea in the listings. This was quite a laborious job considering Alexandria's enormous population, but I instructed the city's registration magistrate to assign several clerks to search, stating there was a rather large lawsuit involved. In another two weeks Solon came to me in triumph with the information. A Penelope Timoclea Philip, Macedonian in origin (a requirement of the registration) resided upstairs over a store she and her husband owned in the agora behind the harbor docks.

At first I thought I might visit the shop, a bookstore which apparently specialized in the sale of reproductions of scrolls of antiquity, a reason why possibly Penelope, whose father had given her a love of ancient literature, might have married this Philip. But then I realized the absurdity of the praefectus of all Egypt wandering into a cheap bookstore near the harbor docks. Instead I instructed Solon to enter the shop as though looking to purchase several copies of ancient scrolls and listen to any conversation that might be useful in the tax case involving the woman's family.

A week later I got Solon's report. It was extraordinary though—as I already knew it had nothing to do with family inheritance and taxes. This is what he told me:

Called The Macedonian, *the store was low class. Only the cheapest papyrus was used in their book scrolls and most of them were not only secondhand but in frayed condition. I pretended to study the scrolls while listening to the conversation between a gross-looking middle-aged man, who seemed to be the proprietor, and two other men, obviously Greek. Three children were dusting the scrolls. Two of the children were blond. The oldest, darker, with a somewhat hooked nose, had a different look. The door to the back room of the store was open.*

The men cast a quick glance at me to reassure themselves I too was Greek. Then one of the two said: "Philip, we came to congratulate you. It's all over the stores down here owned by us. They say you killed a Jew in the recent riots."

"I did my best," the proprietor said in mock modesty.

"Penelope," one of the men called out. "Come to the front. We are here to congratulate you on your husband killing a Jew in the Jewish uprising."

A middle-aged, rather heavy woman with sagging breasts ill-concealed under a cheap cotton dress come in from the back.

"Don't congratulate her. Penelope is a Jew-lover," her husband said coldly.

The woman, apparently the Penelope you inquired about, said sharply, "I am not. I am no Jew-lover. But unlike my husband and you two I don't hate, Jew or no Jew. And don't talk that way in front of the children. They'll get wrong ideas."

"You are too. You are. I know you are, I'm long married to you. Sometimes I even think you may have had a secret affair with a Jew before marrying me. I once heard you even call out in your sleep, 'Tiberius,' though that of course was our former emperor's name and not that of a Jew."

"Isn't that also the name of our wonderful praefectus?" one of the men asked.

"The one who called in the legions to kill the Jews."

"Yes, she's been sleeping with the praefectus," another said to general laughter.

The wife, Penelope, looked down at the floor. "Excuse me," she said. "I've got work to do. I just want to add that my father was a librarian at the Great Library, a learned man, and he taught me that all of us, Greeks, Jews, or fellaheen, were pretty much the same except for education. And my fellow Macedonians, don't forget that though our Alexander was truly the greatest man in history, most Greek learning came from the south of Graecia, from Athens and the Ionian islands. So I've said my bit." And she went back to the rear room.

"By Zeus!" said one of the men. "How can you live with a woman like that? She's a walking encyclopedia."

"That comes," Philip, her husband, said with disgust, "from women being allowed to study. It was better when they stayed in the kitchen." Another added, "In the bed." The other men laughed and nodded assent.

I broke in to Solon's story. "Nothing about taxes or inheritance?" I asked, to continue the fake reason for the investigation.

"Nothing," Solon answered. "But you can tell any court or judge that seeing that store and its contents, there's no money in that family."

"What did you say the wife looked like? She would be the litigant in any legal action," I asked.

"Just another middle-aged woman, overweight, and, as I said, with sagging breasts from suckling her children and a wrinkled, rather sad face. Though almost completely grey-haired, at one time she must have been blond because wisps of yellow hair still stuck out above her ears. I will say that I was struck by her eyes, a really unusual color of green. I fancy she might have been good-looking when young."

"Thanks, Solon," I said. "A good report. We won't follow through on that legal action. It would be a waste of time."

"I agree," he said. "There's nothing there of value."

"Thanks again," I said. "Fine job. I'll see you at the next Monday meeting."

Solon left. I took out a bottle and drank two large glasses of Mareotis wine.

I had in the bottom shelf of my wardrobe a fancy mirror, a highly polished sheet of metal framed with a back decoration showing a satyr chasing a nymph. I took the mirror in hand and, before looking at myself, I said with all the will power I could command, "Don't look at yourself as you think you are. Concentrate on looking at yourself as a stranger would see you."

I put the mirror before my closed eyes, made my mind a blank, and then opened them.

For a fraction of a second I saw myself not as I imagined but as I really looked. I saw a middle-aged man with a heavy head, rather hooked nose, grey hair thinning out, cheeks flushed and spotted from too much wine, creases running down the cheeks to the corners of his mouth, wrinkled forehead, and a rather cruel twist to thin lips. The mirror showed an ugly man with an expression of disdain and power. And most curious, I noticed with a flash that I had begun to look more Roman than Jewish. They say one resembles those persons with whom one is in constant contact, and my features, the twist of my mouth, hooked nose, and balding head, were indeed becoming more Roman in look. And I might add it was somewhat like the faces of the emperors I knew personally, not idealized as on some coins but with the brutal look of men holding and using despotic power.

I collapsed into my armchair and stared at nothing. "Life, life, what is life?" kept running through my mind. "You, Tiberius, an ugly middle-aged man, a cruel-looking Roman administrator. Penelope, a fat lady with sagging breasts and a face sorrowed by hardship.

"What did it all mean? Where did my ambition lead me? I was the last of my family line. I was alone except for respectable subordinates who probably hated me. A heavy drinker, I drank to forget. To forget what? To forget what I did, breaking with my family and community, my loss of the one true love I ever felt, the compromises, the betrayals and lies I used to rise to the top of the Roman bureaucracy, my family all dead because, because . . . I don't want to think about that."

I pulled forward another bottle of wine, savagely pulled out the cork, and drank until I passed out.

XIX

As praefectus of Egypt for four years, with my knowledge of the abuses built into the system when serving as an epistrategus, I remembered the abandonment of whole villages because of injustice. Coming from a family with a business background, I tried to correct the worst abuses. It was difficult because graft was built into and had become a part of the way business was done. Subordinates would agree to correct abuses and then, paid off, would evade action. If it were a question of a dishonest official here or there, something might be done. But when the corruption was an organized part of the government, it was impossible.

I issued edicts. No one could confiscate the crops of farmers or foreclose a legally constituted and maintained mortgage. Public force was forbidden for private gain. Excessive taxes were nullified as was the illegal seizure of farm land. The use of contacts to delay decisions already made was forbidden. Women's rights were to be protected, especially those of helpless widows. And there could be no imprisonment for debt except through legal process.

The curious part is that my attempts at reform, so I was informed by an esteemed scholar from the Great Library, were almost precisely the same reforms attempted by the Ptolemaic empress Cleopatra VII less than a century before in her desperate attempt to rally the country against the Romans.

The purpose of these cruel extractions was obvious and similar to what was going on all throughout the empire. Slaves, after the original purchase, cost nothing to maintain except food and shelter. Therefore the landlords and land speculators wanted to rid the land of free farmers so through holding slaves their profits would be greater. Since the aristocratic landlords controlled the political system, except in such rare cases as my praefecture, the change from freehold farmers to enormous slave-worked estates was a process that could not be reversed.

I tried to fight the corruption that made this process possible. But one person—even a praefectus, especially in a short period—could do little. And I was further limited by any organized resistance which would disrupt the grain shipments to Rome.

It was about that time that I stopped sleeping at night. I drank to sleep and then had such bad dreams that I got up and drank more. But I learned the Roman way of solving this problem: dip a quill in oil and force it down your throat until you heave up what is in the stomach. Yet I aged and looked much older than my years in a relatively short time, living alone without family and close friends. The Jews, knowing my past, hated me for my apostasy and putting down their revolt. The Greeks admired me, but only as a stranger. And the rich in both communities disliked me for my reforms. Also my sex desire slackened with my aging and heavy drinking, and even the finest brothels now gave me little pleasure.

After a life of abominations Emperor Nero was forced to kill himself two years after he appointed me praefectus of Egypt. There was no legitimate Julio-Claudian heir, all having been killed by Nero as threats to his life. Now the generals decided the fate of Rome; whoever controlled the most legions selected the emperor. Divus Claudius and Nero had made a serious mistake in awarding double pay to the praetorian guards when elevated to be emperors. Now these legionnaires, backed by their centurions, thought only of the extra money if they supported the right candidate as the new emperor.

The nineteen months following the death of Nero were chaotic. There were four emperors: Galba for seven months; Otho for four months; Vitellius for eight months; followed by Vespasian, who inaugurated the Flavian Dynasty.

I knew Galba very well, Otho and Vitellius casually. The reason was my attending the Triumph given by Emperor Nero when General Gaius Suetonius Paulinius conquered the Druid fortress of Mona and thus expanded greatly our hold on Britannia. I may add that these Triumphs, to which all the top administrative and military leaders were invited, served as occasions for the emperors to review their appointments, seeing them so rarely in their far-flung posts.

I liked Galba, already an old man, and the feeling was mutual. Indeed, curious as to the pyramids and huge stone carving in the Egyptian desert, Galba had formerly visited me at Alexandria, and as praefectus of the province I had given him a personal tour. I was so sure of his good will on becoming emperor that I had not bothered to resign my post, as was common practice, but continued by issuing *prostagmata*, the royal edicts, in his name.

Galba was of the high nobility on both sides. Losing his wife and two sons, he remained single thereafter, preferring—as was most common in that high circle—young boys. He had a valiant military career in Gallia under Caligula and was appointed step by step governor of Aquitania, military commander in Germania Superior, proconsul of Mauretania (Africa), and finally governor of Hispania Tarraconensis (Nearer Hispania). He also served under Claudius and Nero, being careful not to offend the latter, a policy I too most carefully followed. After the death of Nero the Roman Senate pronounced him Caesar.

As emperor, though personally very rich, Galba made the initial mistake of sending Nero's German praetorian guards back to Germania without an extra recompense for their service, alienating a core of the army. He also ruled by caprice according to moods so no one could fully trust him, and further alienated important sectors of high Roman society by revoking many gifts made by Nero. Above all he incurred the anger of his own legionnaires who had sworn alliance to him as the first troops but received no donatives.

"I choose my soldiers, I do not buy them" was his witty but inappropriate remark, suitable for Roman soldiers of the Republic who were fighting for their country but no longer relevant for foreign mercenaries who now composed a good part of the legion ranks. The German soldiers as a result refused to swear an oath of allegiance other than to the Roman Senate.

Marcus Salvius Otho, governor of Lusitania, a province in the southwest of Hispania, was at first an ally of Galba, supporting his bid to be emperor, but then sensed his own chance for supreme power. I had met Otho at the Triumph for General Paulinius but knew him less well than I did Galba. He was a descendant of very honorable ancestors including princes of Etruria; his great-grandfather already had been a Roman knight. In looks he was very like Emperor Tiberius, many believing he was his son. Short, with weak feet and thin hair, Otho was so vain that he plucked the hair from his body and wore a wig.

Debauched from youth, I was told, Otho became the lover of the beautiful Poppaea but Nero then was attracted and married her, sending Otho to be governor of distant Lusitania. Hating Nero as a result, he thus backed Galba though each of them had the support of only one legion. When Galba, without living issue, was ratified by the Roman Senate, Otho had hoped to be adopted as his heir, only to be shattered by the choice of someone else.

A very rich man, Otho then organized a plot, bribing the praetoriani, the emperor's guards, who as a result murdered Galba.

At the time of Galba's death he was seventy-two, bald, with a hooked nose. I regretted his death though that sentiment was diluted by the rumor that, uncertain of Vespasian's ambitions—whose relations with me were close since our days together in the conquest of Britannia years before—he had sent assassins from Spain to kill him. Indeed, we in the Orient recognized Galba as emperor but, as with the German troops, did not compel out legions to swear the usual oath of loyalty.

In this same period Aulus Vitellius had been hailed emperor by the angry German legions in the north of Europe. Two opposing armies, that in the south supporting Otho and that in the north supporting Vitellius, moved toward each other, met in battle near the Po River and, Otho's forces being defeated, he committed suicide. He was thirty-eight years of age at his death.

Aulus Vitellius I met briefly at the aforementioned Triumph but my friend Vespasian warned me against him as most treacherous. He was right. Vitellius was so despicable in conduct that in a sense he caused Vespasian to become emperor as a reaction to his vileness.

Vitellius, son of a Roman knight and procurator under Divus Augustus, spent his childhood and youth on the island of Capri and was reputed to have been one of the *spintriae*, or boy whores, of Tiberius; this opinion was so common that his nickname was Spintria. A man of that nature was naturally popular with Caligula and even more so with Nero, whose first prizes in harp playing and singing Vitellius arranged.

Being close to these three emperors for his fawning and flattery, Vitellius received the proconsulship of Mauretania, where in two years he stole the gifts and ornaments of many temples. His technique was to substitute tin and copper for the gold and silver objects. In his first marriage, the rich mother ordaining their son as heir, he arranged the boy to be poisoned.

Sent by Galba to rule Germaina Inferior, Vitellius favored to an extraordinary degree the legions stationed there, freeing condemned men, relaxing discipline, and giving gifts. The German troops, twice denied donatives under the previous two emperors—first by Galba and then by Otho—seeing Vitellius so generous, then seized the opportunity and saluted him as emperor. The legions in both provinces of Germania united and the combined force moved south to confront the troops of Otho, which as stated they defeated.

Marching to Rome in triumph with his troops, drunk as usual, Vitellius's first act was to call together several priests and sacrifice to the spirit of "Divus" Nero. At supper that same night he bestowed a knighthood on a favorite male whore. Dividing his time between belly and cruelty he segmented each day into four meals, the fourth being a drinking bout. He put to death by caprice or greed whosoever he desired. Since an oracle had prophesied he would not outlive his mother, Vitellius arranged as well to poison her.

All fighting that involved these three emperors, Galba, Otho, and Vitellius, took place in Europe and the legions in the East were not involved. The cloud of these eastern legions, however, lay thick over the scene though unacknowledged by the combatants. I was friendly with Gaius Licinius Mucianus, *legatus* or military leader of Syria, as well as Vespasian, who controlled the troops in Judaea. We three dominated seven legions, over 40,000 soldiers, as well as an almost equal number of auxiliaries who could be called up if necessary. Nobody as a result wanted to offend us and not one of us was asked to resign our positions by the short-term emperors. And each of these emperors ended weakening his legions through the fighting while ours remained intact.

The family of Flavius Vespasianus, usually shortened to Vespasian, was of obscure origin unlike the noble pedigrees of the aforementioned three emperors. He was born north of Rome, at Realte, five years before the death of Divus Augustus, and thus he was only slightly older than I was. He joined the army and after several small positions was chosen as a praetor, or magistrate, placed in charge of state documents. Marrying a woman of similar obscure background he had two sons, Titus and Domitianus, as well as a daughter who died early.

Under Emperor Claudius he was transferred back to the military and was first sent to Germania, and then to Britannia, where he fought thirty battles and where of course we met. As a reward he was sent as proconsul, a high command, to the province of Mauretania, as had been Vitellius, a position which he held with great dignity.

While traveling later with Emperor Nero he almost lost his life by falling asleep while the emperor was singing. However, Nero recognized his martial abilities and when the Judean revolt broke out he picked Vespasian to put down the rebellion. An additional reason was that Emperor Nero had no fear of a stab for power from Vespasian because of his plebeian background.

The Judean revolt had started out with great success due to the arrogance and stupidity of the local Roman leaders there, both civil and military. The Roman procurator, Gessius Florus, was killed. The rebels struck with initial great force, wiping out some of the Roman contingents in the province, which brought to their side many, if not most, of their compatriots who initially opposed the revolt as being a hopeless dream.

Everything changed with the capable Vespasian in command. To be sure of total control, he brought over from Italy his son Titus, who though only twenty-seven had already seen military service in Germania and Britannia. Vespasian then reinforced his legions by summoning two more from Cilicia and Cappadocia; and Titus, sent to me in Alexandria, brought up another legion. Now, with some 60,000 legionnaires plus auxiliaries, Vespasian struck hard at the rebels, overwhelming them in a slow but steady campaign which kept his army together to avoid ambushes and killed without mercy not only the Judean fighters but a good part of the general population as well. It was at Jotapata, near Sepphoris, where the Romans captured Josephus, whose story I will shortly recount.

After a short rest from the summer heat, staying with King Agrippa II at Caesarea Philippi, the capital of that king's small kingdom, Vespasian and Titus continued their triumphant march south, destroying city after city and depopulating the land to the point that Judaea could never again be considered an independent province; and besides the hundreds of thousands killed, some 31,000 Judean slaves were auctioned off by the Romans. Except for some isolated towns, all Galilee was soon under the Roman heel, as was Peraea (east of Judaea) and a good part of the heartland of Judaea. Vespasian continued to move south, determined to take Jerusalem and end the revolt. It had taken him some eighteen months to reduce, and in a practical sense, destroy the country.

It may be useful to turn back time to the start of the revolt in order to show that Roman arrogance was met by blind fanaticism on the part of the Judean leaders, which made the clash inevitable. The situation in Jerusalem had become more and more threatening since King Agrippa I died and Emperor Claudius reduced Judaea to a Roman province under the administration of greedy procurators. Gessius Florus in that position was especially rapacious, including demanding money from the Temple treasure, which under the *Pax Romana* was against Roman law. The city was in an uproar but Florus, devoid of common sense, insisted on the arrest of those protesting. The Jewish priests said they did not know the ringleaders and that the riots had been a popular mass protest. Florus then ordered his troops to loot the upper market, killing some 4,000 Judeans, including an almost unheard of act, those with Roman citizenship.

Just at this time King Agrippa II was on the way back to his kingdom after visiting Alexandria to congratulate me on my appointment as praefectus of Egypt. He met his sister Princess Berenice at Jerusalem, and she is the one who later told me of these events.

Procurator Gessius Florus had sent to Caesarea for reinforcements, where they met a Jewish delegation going there to protest Florus's actions. Among the Jews were some hotheads who mocked the legionnaires. The latter promptly attacked the unarmed delegation, killing scores. When the Roman soldiers entered Jerusalem they were met in the narrow streets by a hail of stones, forcing them to retreat.

Florus, who had caused the uprising through his greed, was frightened that an adverse report might be sent to Emperor Nero, threatening his position. He sent a message to Cestius Gallus, now governor of the imperial province of Syria, who ruled over Judaea as well, blaming everything on the Judeans. The Jewish leaders countered with the exact opposite in a report they delivered to Gallus, who sent down a staff member to investigate both claims. After a brief tour of the city, he reported that no one side could be blamed. Gallus decided to ignore the matter.

King Agrippa II and his sister Berenice remained in Jerusalem. They resolved to appeal for moderation. Agrippa asked the people to assemble beneath the Herodian Palace, where he could speak before a huge open space below the terrace.

Berenice told me it was a very clever speech. Agrippa reviewed all the peoples of the world who had succumbed to the Roman legions, most with populations far greater than Judaea, running north to south from Britannia to Mauretania and west to east from Hispania to Lesser Armenia. He listed those countries with greater resources who could not withstand Rome. He referred to the total of twenty-eight legions, or about 170,000 soldiers, plus auxiliaries, who could be called up to ravage a city like Jerusalem, where the normal population was little more than 100,000 persons and that figure included old men, women, and children. He pointed out that almost all Judaea except Jerusalem and two desert fortresses had already fallen to the Romans. Any such revolt, Agrippa stated with exorable logic, was both stupid and suicidal. In an appeal to Jewish religious sentiment he emphasized that it would be impossible for Rome to create such a huge empire without the providence of Yahweh. Putting down the hopes of some that Parthia, the enemy of Rome to the east of Judaea, would take advantage of the situation, Agrippa also pointed out that the recent treaty between Parthia and Rome negotiated by Nero had a clause that each would come to the aid of the other in case of war. His final touch was to remind the rebels that to oppose Rome they would have to fight on the Sabbath, which would surely deprive them of divine assistance.

Berenice said that beforehand she and her brother Agrippa had clenched in the palms of their hands a powder that irritated the eyes and, ending Agrippa's speech when he referred to the horrors of war, they in a quick motion rubbed the powder on their eyelids and thus burst into tears.

The great speech had a momentary effect until the fanatics shouted defiance. Agrippa was insulted and even stoned. He retreated into the Herodian Palace and then left for his kingdom in the Galilee. It was not only that the extremists had won; from my own experience as a former procurator of Judaea almost twenty years before, I knew the basic problem. It was that these fanatics considered themselves as leaders of the unique Chosen People and that against such illogic nothing could persuade them to believe they would be beaten. And so their fate was cast.

I tell this incident to justify my position in the following siege of Jerusalem. Being now a Roman military commander in spirit as well as fact I also took consolation in the thought that my Uncle Philo would have also opposed the Judean revolt. I could still remember lines from one of his dialogues, which impressed me greatly as a youth: "Are there not certain men who are more savage and treacherous than boars, spiders, and asps, men whose treachery and hostility can be escaped only by mollifying and propitiating them?" He obviously would have meant the Judean procurators who bilked the people, which, however, was less suicidal than a hopeless revolt. I was glad that Philo at age sixty-five, twelve years before the outbreak of the rebellion, had been struck down and killed by a horse and carriage on the Canopus Way in Alexandria while absentmindedly walking to the Great Library.

In the meantime there was chaos in Jerusalem, greatly swollen by unrepentant rebels and refugees from the Galilee, as well as those who had come to celebrate the holiday of Passover—the Jews passing under Moses through the waters of the Red Sea—which occurred at that time. The city was rent by factions, the Sadducees, the rich and the moderates seeking peace no matter how humiliating to save their Holy Temple and the city itself from destruction; while most of the Pharisees, the country peasants fleeing to the city and the city poor clamored for continued resistance. To add to this internal anarchy, the radicals had broken up into three factions, killing each other. Many thousands were murdered in this internal warfare, with the food supplies running out. To complete the lunacy one faction even set fire to the grain storage area, intentionally or not we will never know, which had been set up in case of such a siege.

Vespasian, approaching Jerusalem, was unsure whether to mass a frontal attack or starve the city into submission. He decided on the former when news was brought him that Nero had been forced to commit suicide. Vespasian then suspended the campaign; as was Roman law, he could not continue without orders from a new emperor. It was in a way unfortunate for the ultimate fate of the city, as Princess Berenice later told me, because it confirmed the view of the Zealots, who thus gained strength, that Yahweh had intervened to save Jerusalem. And this of course hardened their resolve.

In Rome meantime it was the end of the Juilo-Claudian imperial reign because, as mentioned before, Nero had killed off any of the royal family who could be a threat to him. This was the period of a year and one half of four emperors.

Vespasian's reputation was greatly advanced in the Judean campaign, aided by his son Titus, for his imposition of discipline on the legions grouped under him as well as his courage when he entered the fray personally and indeed received several arrows in his shield. Perhaps most of all he was admired by the legions and the Roman Senate for his dignity and modesty, so unlike what they had to face under the three short-term former emperors. His future conduct as emperor I cannot comment on for by that time I was very sick. Yet it was already obvious to me that he would make a splendid leader. And as I look back I also think a reason he favored me, aside from my control of two legions and their auxiliaries in Egypt, was that somehow he equated his advance from an obscure background with a rather similar situation I had in my ascent to become praefectus of that country. Whether he was aware of my Jewish birth and Julio-Claudian name by adoption and not gens I do not know.

Instead of returning to Rome Vespasian stayed in the East, avoiding the internecine wars among the legions after the death of Nero. Although wisely recognizing each of the three short-term emperors, the murder of Galba, the suicide of Otho, and the violent factional fighting about Vitellius made him seriously think of the possibility of becoming emperor himself.

Originally there was tension between the military commander Mucianus at Antiochia in Syria, of noble origin, and plebeian Vespasian, the former believing he should have been appointed to stamp out the Judean revolt. But the relation mended when Mucianus, without children, took a liking to Titus. I had no problem with either Mucianus or Vespasian, staying in Egypt and in control of the all-important grain shipments to Rome.

Events moved rapidly. Together sharing contempt for Vitellius, the three of us got together for secret talks at Caesarea. It was agreed that Vespasian would be our candidate for emperor. We swore a mutual oath of fidelity. Mucianus, usually solemn, laughed at our parting and said, "*Summa sedes non capit duos*," a well-known line from Roman folklore, i.e., "There's only room for one at the top." Vespasian and I smiled. It was true. We were committed. Probing our centurions we found them enthusiastic, naturally expecting a reward for their support.

I decided to take the first step. It had been slightly less than a century since the start of the Julio-Claudian Dynasty and each emperor after Divus Augustus—Tiberius, Caligula, Claudius, and Nero—had been to a good extent more depraved and less able. The people as well as the legions had lost affection for the dynasty, as well as the short-term emperors who followed and, when on July 1 in Alexandria I announced my support for Vespasian as the new emperor, my two legions and auxiliaries without hesitation swore an oath of allegiance to him.

Vespasian came to Alexandria and with festivities organized in his honor by me was enthusiastically welcomed by the Greeks who, being violently anti-Jewish, approved with delight Vespasian's depopulation of most of Judaea. And of course our relation was cemented by my being his host and initial supporter.

Within two weeks this was followed by similar oaths of allegiance by the legions in Syria. By late August the seven Danubian legions in eastern Germania did the same.

Mucianus with four legions started moving overland from Syria toward Rome and the Danubian legions under their commander, Antonius Primus, marched south and arrived at Rome first. A tremendous battle between the legions of Primus and those of Vitellius resulted in victory for the former and Vitellius was even abandoned by his praetorian guard. The victorious legionnaires found him hiding with a girdle full of gold coins. Pleading for his life he was brought to the Forum, dragged through the *sacra via*, and killed by a series of small strokes. Then he was thrown into the Tiber River. He was fifty-seven at the time, exceedingly tall, with a red face swollen by wine and a huge potbelly. Rome was well rid of him.

Mucianus, arriving with his legions only a few days later, was furious at being deprived of the victory and a clash between the two armies was only averted by Vespasian giving the two commanders great rewards. I, under orders from Vespasian, remained in Alexandria with my two legions to be sure no unrest would break out in the East.

The rest is standard history. Vespasian was confirmed emperor by the Roman Senate. He then went to Rome—he had stayed away while all this was taking place—and left his son Titus to capture Jerusalem.

Vespasian's trust in me was obvious. Indeed, he celebrated his advent to power on the date of July 1, when my legions swore allegiance to him—*dies imperii*—and not as was protocol on the date of his confirmation by the Roman Senate. This showed openly that the supreme power had now shifted from the senate to the legions. Since Titus was only thirty and with limited background in warfare, Vespasian, familiar with my military history, instructed him to bring me in as chief of staff, as I had been under Commander Corbulo. Though Titus, as son of the emperor was of course *dux*, commander-in-chief, I was therefore head of the council of the generals pursuing the war in Judaea, or more technically, *primus inter pares*, first among equals.

I had attained the peak of power for a non-Roman by birth; or better put—since my father had been granted Roman citizenship by Divus Augustus—the peak of power for an Egyptian in the Roman Empire.

Titus (Titus Flavius Vespasianus) was short, as usual with a big belly from food and wine, and like Nero he could sing and play the harp as well as compose verses in both Latin and Greek. He loved music and literature and was an expert at shorthand. He also had a prodigious memory and would often walk among the legionnaires and call out by name one or another to their amazement and delight. Titus had read what Roman writers wrote about the Jews before coming to the East and would quote with zeal the philosopher Seneca as describing with contempt "the customs of this very evil race," as well as the renowned Cicero, who attacked their "barbarous superstitions, incompatible with the glory of Rome."

Though to me Titus was always generous and open to advice (I served as a sort of foster father), he had a streak of cruelty which showed in his pleasure while crucifying captive prisoners. He was very courageous and indeed reckless: while serving under his father Vespasian in the early days of the Judean war two years before, he had a horse killed under him; and we commanders had to urge him not to take one of the night watches at Jerusalem, where the rebels would slip through the gates in the dark and kill Roman sentries. A tie between us as well was Titus's infatuation with Princess Berenice who, as I have related, had been married at a very young age to my dead brother Marcus.

Princess Berenice herself had a colorful life. Considered one of the most beautiful women of our time and very wealthy as well—her diamonds were the envy of Rome—after Marcus's death Berenice married her paternal uncle Herod Pollio, king of Chalcis, a small state in northern Galilee. Leaving him, she then married Polemon, king of Pontus and Cilicia, who had himself circumcised at her insistence. She abandoned him in turn and rejoined her brother at his father's small kingdom of Chalcis, a Roman sycophant to the point of calling himself *philokaisar, plus, philoromaios*, i.e., "Lover of Caesar, Dutiful, Lover of Rome." It was claimed that Berenice had a long illicit relation with him. Finally she seduced Titus, though some ten years older than he, and stayed with him at our Roman camp during the siege of Jerusalem. Later, though then sick and secluded, I heard that Berenice followed Titus to Rome after the war and he was so infatuated that he would have married her but for the united opposition of the Imperial Council, with memories of Cleopatra, to an Oriental princess. Amazingly, despite her dissolute life, she remained a religious Jewess and actually once made a pilgrimage barefoot in Jerusalem to plead for mercy toward the rebels in the early stages of the revolt.

The obstinate resistance of those rebels of Jerusalem made no sense, as I related. To begin with, Judaism was what was called a *religio licita*, a permitted religion, one recognized by the Roman state. Judaea was being attacked rather as a rebellious province than for religious reasons. In fact, during the entire war those practicing the rites of that religion at Rome, of whom there were quite a number, some with very distinguished positions, were not bothered. There were a few exceptions elsewhere, such as the cities of the Decapolis, to the east of Judaea, as well as at Damascus, where some 11,000 Jews were rounded up and had their throats slit. But such horrors were not authorized by the Roman authorities.

Nowhere as well was it held against Princess Berenice, her brother King Agrippa II and his Jewish troops, nor indeed me, whose origins Vespasian might have known, that we came from a Jewish background. Indeed, the province of Judaea had been treated better than most other conquered countries. As a buttress against the Parthian enemy directly to the east the Judeans were granted a number of unusual concessions: for examples, the right to observe the Sabbath, to refuse military service, and to substitute prayers for the emperor in place of participation in the imperial cult. No other subjugated people were granted such concessions.

The greed of the Roman procurators before the revolt was indeed a factor, the last, that of Gessius Florus, being particularly venal. But truth to say, all procurators throughout the empire were more or less the same: the reason they hungered for and received their posts was to milk the populace. And if they carried it too far the emperor recalled them or ordered them to commit suicide. This was not so infrequent.

The Judean resistance at Jerusalem, lasting a bit more than four months, was like a turtle trying to evade the stamp of an elephant. There were already in Judaea three Roman legions, the 5th, the 10th, and the 15th. To these were added the 12th, parts of the 3rd and 22nd; twenty cohorts of allied soldiers and eight squadrons from the vassal states; 5,000 horsemen from King Agrippa II, who led his men personally; and troops from Parthia and Nabatea. Over 100,000 soldiers were in the attacking force, not counting auxiliaries.

To the contrary, Judaea was a small country of some 2,500,000 persons now much reduced by the campaigns of Vespasian over two years of warfare. Though greatly swollen by refugees and persons coming to celebrate the holiday of Passover, we had far more experienced soldiers attacking Jerusalem than there were defenders. And if necessary we could call for more legions as well as auxiliaries. The Judean resistance was simply madness. This was even more true when we learned from a deserter that the combined rebel forces led by the first three and then two fanatics had no military experience and could mount no more than 20,000 men, most of whom had never been in battle.

Actually, Titus could have taken Jerusalem simply by starvation. But he wanted a Triumph along the *via sacra* in Rome, the supreme compliment to a conquering commander, with a parade of triumphant soldiers and forlorn captives. So he insisted on the conquest of the city in military fashion.

At the first meeting of our commanders' council, most of whom I knew from other campaigns, there was an unknown face which somehow looked familiar. He stared at me uncertainly. "You will excuse me, Commander," he said, "I have spent my entire military career in Germania, and you command legions from Egypt, but I think I know you."

"Tiberius Julius Alexander," I said rather curtly. I knew from experience that those aristocratic Roman commanders despised Egyptians, though in my case they dared not show it.

"Tiberius Julius, my cousin," he said with delight. "We are kinsmen of the Julio-Claudian clan. Remember? Antonia, mother of Divus Claudius, recommended that you stay with me, which you did when you came to Rome as a young man on business for her estates in Egypt. I am Antonio Julius Lepidus, your old comrade and roommate."

With a rush a hundred memories ran through my head. This was my dear friend from youth, Antonio, now fat and balding. And a commander, as he had always dreamed to be.

Those happy days of youth! Tears came to my eyes and while the other commanders looked on in amazement I threw my arms around him in a massive hug and kissed both his cheeks. "Welcome, welcome, Antonio," I kept repeating. It was the first touch of human sympathy I had felt in years. In the conversation ensuing I also noticed what seemed a more marked difference from the other commanders. They had thought of me as an upstart Egyptian who miraculously had ascended to power in the military. "A Julio-Claudian! A friend of Antonia, mother of Divus Claudius! So that's how he got the name Tiberius Julius," I could almost hear them thinking. "Here indeed Emperor Nero was following the aristocratic rules of imperial Rome." The commanders from then on showed me a respect deeper than due to my leadership of the War Council.

Antonio Julius Lepidus changed my life at our camp outside Jerusalem. The years fell away and we were almost prankish with each other. Both of us were addicted to red wine at dinner as well as afterward, and where before I had been serious and guarded, with Antonio—as is with friends from youth—I softened up. He reminded me of ribald songs he had taught me; I reminded him of trips to brothels where we bet each other as to who could make love quicker, and more often. The camaraderie spread; and Titus himself joined in bawdy tales about the aristocratic ladies, married and unmarried, with whom he had slept at Rome. Our Council, though serving in a war, was the most pleasant I had served on.

On one thing I insisted, as Council head, despite Antonio's disgust. Pleading seniority, I stated he should not take night sentry duty, which could be dangerous because there were always Judean fanatics willing to die if they could kill a Roman, especially a Roman commander. Antonio made such a fuss, insisting he wanted to share all danger "as a true Roman" and kept complaining until I agreed if he would be accompanied by several legionnaires. Finally we settled on one; until the day I die I will regret the decision. But that tragic event came later.

XX

At this point I would like to digress to mention an interesting man, probably the most interesting Judean of my time after Agrippa I, grandson of Herod the Great. He was Joseph ben Matthias, called Josephus by the Romans, and was an advisor on Titus's staff. This was how I learned about Josephus.

Of noble Jewish origin—indeed his mother was of Hasmonean descent and his father was a priest, as he himself became—Josephus showed from the start outstanding ability and, what was equally important, an extraordinary talent (as had King Agrippa I) to ingratiate himself with everyone by his personal charm. At an early age, attracted by the Essenes, he spent three years in the desert living as a hermit. Then, forsaking Essene practices, he first moved back to Jerusalem and then when twenty-six went to Rome where, as was I, he became dazzled by Roman splendor.

Going back to Judaea, his heart was divided between the forces of rebellion and those of submission. At the age of thirty the Jerusalem high priests, initially in charge of the revolutionary forces, sent him as the general—though totally without military experience—to lead the rebels in the Galilee. The results could easily have been foreseen and the area, itself tepid about rebelling against Rome, collapsed in no time before Vespasian's legions. The stronghold of Jotapata held out with Josephus in command until only forty soldiers were still alive, hiding with Josephus in a cave.

At this point the cunning of Josephus first became apparent. The men preferred suicide to crucifixion or slavery and lots were drawn by numbered markings on slips of papyrus as to the order of suicide, the numbers held by Josephus, who gave himself the last number. When all but one soldier was left, Josephus convinced him that the two should surrender to the Romans.

About to be sent in chains to Rome, Josephus then again showed his foxlike mind. Brought before Vespasian he prophesized that he, Vespasian, would shortly become emperor, followed by his two sons. He stated that the Judeans had been mistaken, that the Messiah had indeed come yet he was not of their people but rather a Roman, that is, Vespasian himself.

The commander being a typical superstitious Roman, Josephus referred to all the positive prophecies he had learned while living in Rome, portents shown by the flight of birds circling the building where Vespasian was quartered, jagged lightning overhead, and the unexpected growth of saplings from what seemed dead roots of trees.

A crowning touch, Josephus stated that he had seen a large eagle perched on the cornice of a ruined building facing the entry to Vespasian's headquarters. Then he quoted an old Eastern prophecy, "there shall come out of Judaea those who were to be lords of the world," and this, Josephus pointed out, obviously referred to Vespasian and his sons.

The Roman commander, though dubious at first, finally was enchanted by these portents, particularly when viewing the demise of the short-term emperors. His view of the future was reinforced because earlier he had entered the temple of the Egyptian god Serapis, where he had a vision that he was given sacred herbs and holy garlands. He released Josephus and accepted him as advisor in the war against Judaea, which was in limbo for two years after Nero's forced suicide.

The advent of Vespasian as emperor fulfilled the prophecy. Vespasian was convinced that Josephus was in touch with the spirits and transferred him to the staff of his son Titus when the latter marched against the holdout city of Jerusalem. Josephus was then excommunicated by the priests in Jerusalem.

I myself distrusted Josephus although I must admit that despite all he continued to consider himself a devoted Jew. I never could understand that because to me, at least for a person on the staff of Titus, he had to make a choice: either Rome or Jerusalem, for the two were incompatible. I also happened to know he was a gifted writer because Titus, naturally distrustful of a believing Jew so high in his camp, had me read the letters of Josephus before they were dispatched: as mentioned, after two years as procurator of Judaea I had learned Aramaic and found the literary style of Josephus excellent. To sum up, in my opinion he was an excellent example of the adage, "better a living dog than a dead lion."

There were those in Jerusalem who opposed the rebellion. A revered rabbi, Yohanan ben Zakkai, went over to the Roman side. I was told later he became the hero of many rabbis after the war in separating their religion from the national state of Judaea. The priests Zefania and Herod sought refuge with King Agrippa II at his kingdom. Chanania, the richest Jew, vanished, as did Zebulon, the secretary of state. Many of the Essenes fled to caves outside the city, and Yeshuites, now sometimes called Christianoi, the Greek term, opposed the war and crossed the river Jordan to Pella in order to escape the conflict.

We had rather a clear idea of what was going on in the city since rich deserters bribed the Roman night sentries to leave and then bought their freedom by paying us more with what was probably Temple treasury gold. I can give a brief overview as I heard and lived it; whether it agrees with what Josephus will write in his history of the war I cannot say.

Early successes in the rebellion hardened the forces of the Zealots. The high priests, the noble Sadducees, tried to moderate the revolution but to no avail, for the leaders of the revolt did a very clever thing. They burned the municipal archives, which held the mortgages and legal papers involving loans and property ownership, thus enlisting the enthusiasm of the city masses and the farmers seeking refuge. The revolution thus became a revolt against the rich, who in the start of the war then fled the city or were hunted down and killed. The fight was thereby transformed into a poor people's struggle as much as a religious uprising. The rebels then set fire to the mansion of the high priest Ananias and to the Hasmonean Palace.

The irrevocable break occurred when the trapped Roman soldiers, sent by Procurator Florus to put down the early stages of the revolt, offered to give up their arms if allowed to leave the city. The insurgents agreed but after the troops did this the rebels killed them. News of this perfidy was sent back to Rome and a massive counterblow was then organized. It was at that point indeed when Emperor Nero appointed Vespasian to launch full-scale war.

Jerusalem initially was controlled by three rebel groups. By a ruse the followers of one were forced to surrender, reducing them to two, Yohanan of Gischala and Shimon ben Giora. Shimon had a larger number of soldiers but Yohanan's supporters held the Upper City and could cast down missiles upon Shimon's men. Both rebels shared the same violent views and thus it was a fight not of principle but rather for supreme control of the revolution. This was when the two rivals as stated before, setting fires to burn out one another, destroyed the warehouses holding the grain to withstand a long siege and thus effectively ruined whatever chance of success they may have had.

The arrival of huge Roman battering rams to break down the three walls circling the city brought a measure of sanity to the two leaders who, frightened at last, agreed to a truce, an agreement whereby each retained his position within the city.

Our Roman soldiers, working under the shelter of three enormous ironclad towers rolled to the city walls, and which reached above the wall heights, breached one wall after the other, protected from the insurgents by archers atop the rams. Starvation soon assaulted the defenders, a more formidable enemy than arrows. The city folk panicked and tried to flee but Yohanan and Shimon declared that anyone attempting to leave would be killed. Titus, in disgust at the resistance, countered by building a wall encircling Jerusalem and thus doubly trapped those within. He then sent Josephus in one last attempt to arrange a surrender, thinking that finally the rebels could see their end was near. This was particularly important for the turncoat because his family was trapped in the city.

Josephus, in what amounted to a repetition of the earlier speech of King Agrippa II at the outset of the revolt, implored the defenders to give up, stating Titus had promised him none would be punished except the leaders. Josephus pointed out the military prowess of the Roman troops, their greatly superior numbers, Roman control over the whole world which showed the favor of Yahweh, and emphasized that the rebels' lack of food had already led to famine and disease. He further stated that fighting on the Sabbath, a sacrilege, had lost them any help of Yahweh. For those Jews who hoped for Parthian entry on their side, Parthia to the east of Judaea being a traditional enemy of Rome, Josephus added that under terms of the treaty recently concluded, King Vologasus of Parthia had already sent mounted archers to help put down the revolt, and even their fellow Judean, King Agrippa II, had sent squadrons of cavalry to aid Titus.

Josephus of course was right. But nothing could break the stubborn resistance. Titus became so angry he set up a line of a hundred crosses facing the city and crucified each day a new set of captives.

What amazed me was the stoicism of some of the crucified. Several even spat at us as we passed. One very young man, barely in his teens, even cried at me in Aramaic, never dreaming I understood, "Pour out thy wrath on the heathen, Yahweh! O Yahweh." My throat tightened but I continued walking as though ignorant of his curse.

Then the Judean rebel soldiers seized the food of women, children and the old to retain their strength and the corpses daily thrown over the walls increased. Defenders who still managed to bribe their way out told us the rebels were now reduced to eating their shoes, dung, old hay, and even the leather from their shields. A deserter also told us a story hard to believe, namely that one women boiled her infant to eat the corpse! And still the Zealots fought on with the hallucinatory belief that Yahweh would come to their aid as He had against the Assyrians who hundreds of years before were struck by a plague when assaulting Jerusalem and forced to leave; and of course always referring to the Maccabees who beat the greatly superior Greek forces.

War begets cruelty and cruelty begets more cruelty. A legionnaire noticed a deserter fishing through his excrement to find gold coins he had swallowed. The soldiers then began to rip open the stomachs and intestines of deserters to find gold; it was claimed a thousand persons were ripped apart in one day, often without bothering to cut their throats first. Defenders peering down from the shattered walls saw this and the flow of deserters stopped; they preferred starvation and martyrdom to such a hideous fate.

The stench of the dead lay on and outside the city like a filthy blanket. The rebels flung corpses out, there being no place in the city to bury them, and at night hyenas and wild dogs came to feast. The legionnaires draped cloths over their faces to cut down the stench and possible disease while slipping on the half-chewed human carcasses littering the ground both outside and within the breached walls. Several horses slipped in the slime, fell, and had to be killed because of broken legs.

The end came by accident. Very early in the morning a squad of soldiers noticed the rebel guards, atop the Antonia Fortress, a holdout building, seemed absent or were asleep. Two legionnaires scaled its wall, slit the throats of the sleeping guards, and one, a trumpeter, sounded a rallying call. Hearing the trumpeter, Titus ordered the whole army into assault. Immediately behind the Antonia Fortress was the Temple and both sides knew its fall meant the end of resistance. After three days of savage fighting the defenders of the Temple entry were crushed. However, the last remnant of the rebels entrenched themselves within the Temple, built like a fortress itself, and Titus, frustrated, ordered its outer gates set on fire. But the inner gates stood firm.

Before launching the final assault Titus called an emergency Council of War, attended by the commanders, the new praefectus of Egypt, and the proconsul for Judaea. Several centurions were there as well but they had no vote. Of course I did. The question was whether to spare or destroy the Temple.

Previous to the meeting, knowing the agenda, I approached Princess Berenice and from some lingering impulse of my past asked her in the time-honored way of such matters with women to convince her lover Titus to spare the Temple.

The strategy worked as I knew it had that morning before the Council when she winked at me. After heated discussion at the meeting the Council split until Titus, my voting with him, declared it would reflect greatly on the might and magnanimity of conquering Rome to save the Temple, a building renowned for its splendid architecture.

At the emergency meeting I noticed my dear friend Antonio was not there, which was most peculiar. After the vote I inquired as to whether he was sick; the water had become so polluted by corpses that we all had bouts of dysentery. I was met with eyes cast down.

"Where is General Antonio Julius Lepidus?" I demanded, a chill running down my spine. Finally one of the other commanders said, "Bring in the legionnaire who was with him on last night's watch."

A few minutes later the soldier, haggard and frightened, came into our Council room, dragged by two other legionnaires who held his arms.

I wasted no word. "Where is the general you accompanied last night?"

The legionnaire looked down, went even more pale, and said nothing. I noticed that Titus, who knew our close friendship, was watching me.

"Where is your commander?" I snarled and, almost overcome, took out my belt dagger and held it to his throat. He finally spoke, almost in a whimper.

"It was about four o'clock in the morning when, returning from our nightly circuit of the walls, from out of the dark four rebels jumped at us."

He stopped.

"Yes?" I queried with a sinking heart.

"I . . . I lost my nerve," the legionnaire stammered. "There were four of them and they all had swords. I . . . I ran. I ran to a low hill nearby and turned to look. My commander had refused to run but took out his sword and was fighting the four men."

"And you?" I asked, with blood rushing to my head.

"I . . . I watched. My general fought hard. He refused to try and run. Finally one rebel circled, stabbing him in the back. He fell and . . . and they stabbed him in the heart. The blood spurted from his chest . . . and he died.

"The four men spit on him and cutting off his head sang what seemed like a victory chant whose only word being repeated sounded like 'Halleyuya,' which must mean something in their barbaric tongue."

I stood there paralyzed. No one spoke. Finally I faced the soldier, who was being held up from collapsing by the others.

"Soldier," I said sarcastically, "did you train to be a legionnaire?"

"Yes sir," he whimpered.

"Do you recall being taught that when two soldiers were in a difficult situation they automatically turned back to back to protect each other?"

"Yes sir," he whispered.

"And you not only did not do that, you fled, you fled from helping a Roman commander whose pride and nobility would not let him flee. Since," I continued sarcastically, "you presumably speak Latin, I am sure you know the military proverb *Potius mori quam foedari*, and yet you preferred against all we Romans hold dear, the very reverse, dishonor before death."

The legionnaire stared at the floor and said nothing.

I looked at Titus. He guessed what was in my mind and nodded yes.

"Where do you come from, you scum?" I asked.

"Velletri," he whimpered.

"You know of course what happens to a Roman traitor?"

"No, no," he whimpered again.

"Since you are almost a Roman, born so close to our glorious Capitol, I will grant you one favor as a traitor. You will be crucified upside down so death will come sooner. Now soldiers, take the scum away. I want him crucified immediately."

"No, no!" he screamed.

I looked down at the two guards and pointed to the door. "Immediately," I said again. Then, while Titus and the other commanders watched, still silent, I went to the next-door lavatory and vomited. "My last human tie to the world is gone," I kept thinking.

I went back to the Council. Still no one spoke. I turned to Titus. "Sir, do you mind if I leave?"

"Go ahead," he said kindly. "I understand."

I went to our food and liquor store and bought three bottles of good red wine. Then I returned to my quarters, stripped to my skin except for undergarments, removed the corks of the three bottles, and started to drink.

I have no recollection of the next two days. When at last I got up, drenched in vomit and urine and thirsty for water and hungry for food, my undergarments wet with excrement, one thought kept revolving in my mind: my brother, my uncle, my father, my mother, and now my only friend—one after the other—dead. Was I cursed? Was I cursed, or as an epicurean should I think it all coincidence? Or was there more, more than I could see, something I had done which involved me in their deaths?

"Ridiculous." The word came into my head. "I am not responsible for my best friend's death. It was accidental. I am not superstitious. I am a rational man. I certainly had nothing to do with the death of my brother Marcus, killed by Arabs in the Egyptian desert. The fact that my mother was killed when I ordered the legions to put down the Jewish riots in Alexandria was not my fault. My Uncle

Philo was old when run down in an accident at Alexandria. The death of my father in Parthia while I was in command of part of General Corbulo's military invasion when we crossed into Greater Armenia had nothing to do with me."

In our mansion at home in Alexandria we had a parchment attached to the wall on which an artist had painted the Judgment of Solomon, in which that king decides to whom the child belongs in the conflict of two women. It fascinated me as a boy. Suddenly the painting rose before my eyes and I could see King Solomon leering at me. Or was it King Solomon? Or was it rather that dim figure behind the king, enshrouded high in a corner, that awesome figure leering at me?

I smashed the last half-filled bottle against the floor. A piece of glass cut my naked foot and the blood oozed out. I wrapped a cloth around the cut. "Fool! I know I am not a superstitious fool," I said a second time. "We are all born a certain way and we all have to die, but there is no preordained order of events. Perhaps I am more a stoic than an epicurean but I refuse to accept any relation of my choices in life to the deaths of those close to me.

"Silly, silly fool," I exclaimed out loud but I shuddered. I washed, bathed the foot wound, dressed, and went to the usual afternoon meeting of the Council of Commanders. They greeted me as though I had not missed two days. Titus even came over and patted me on the back.

"Titus, you have been too lenient with these fanatics," I said. "Erect a second row of crosses and double the crucifixions so they will understand the might of Rome."

"If we can find the wood," he said, laughing. "The area has been stripped. But I'll try."

And so we doubled the daily crucifixions. And once a day I went out and watched with a degree of pleasure the dying agonies of those rebels. Nor did any other of our cruelties bother me. The last remnants of my Jewish religious training had left me.

I went to Titus at the next Council meeting. "I have a favor, a great favor to ask."

"What is that?" he asked.

"While I stayed with Commander Antonio Julius Lepidus at Rome as a young man at the request of Antonia Nero Drusus, mother of Emperor Claudius—as you know, Antonio and I were of Julio-Claudian kinship—we visited together the great Mausoleum where Julius Caesar and Divus Augustus rest, their ashes held in gold vases with other members of their gens. I promised Antonio that if ever he were killed fighting for the Rome he so loved that I would arrange for his ashes to rest in that sacred Mausoleum. I will pay all the expenses, including the cost of the gold vase."

Titus looked at me a bit in admiration and, I think, a bit astonished. At the mention of those high aristocratic names he nodded vigorously. "You won't pay anything. It will be paid for from the Temple gold we have taken, a divine retribution from Jupiter."

And so it was done. The body and severed head of Antonio were burned according to the ancient rites of Rome, the ashes collected, packaged with care, and sent by Titus to his father, now Emperor Vespasian, with my request and the appropriate money. I kissed the package. *Ultimum vale*, I said, tears in my eyes, "Good-bye forever," I was so integrated into my Roman guise that I felt not a bit guilty pretending to be of the Julio-Claudian kinship rather than an Egyptian adopted into that clan. I even thought as the flames ate Antonio's flesh and bones, "I don't believe in you, Jupiter, but if I am wrong, thank you." I had fulfilled my pledge to Antonio, one of the few things in my life I felt totally good about.

I did have another unhappy experience shortly thereafter. At the end of the siege, the three walls taken and Jerusalem at our mercy, I was riding my horse through the ruins and came to the legionnaires trying to break down the heavy inner Temple doors, so stout they would not yield. One soldier had lit a faggot and was about to throw it through a low window. I knew from my two years as procurator of Judaea that the building interior was lined with cedar wood and he could ignite a huge fire inside. I told the legionnaire to put down the flaming wood. He looked at me and said, "I got no such instructions from my centurion." Furiously I replied, "That was the decision of the War Council. I could have you crucified for your disobedience."

At that he dropped the burning faggot while I noticed his fellow legionnaires move away from him.

Then I was astonished. "Commander," the soldier said, looking me in the eye, "I come from Rome. I am a true Roman of the 10th legion, the Fretensis, quartered originally in Messina. I am not a mercenary from a conquered country. My brother and I volunteered; our family had a good-sized farm outside Rome but we lost it to the rich speculators who could work slaves and undercut the prices of our crops. So my brother and I joined the army. We were inseparable.

"Eight days ago we set up ladders to clamber to the top of the second wall, which had refused to break under the blows of our battering rams. Always the first, my brother climbed and . . . and then" the soldier stopped as his throat tightened, and after a pause continued, "those monsters poured boiling oil down on the legionnaires climbing the ladders." He stopped again and gulped. "My brother fell and lay on the ground screaming in agony. I went up to him and said, 'Claudio, this is your brother. Do you hear me?'

"'Yes, yes,' he mumbled through burnt lips. 'I can't stand it. Kill me, kill me. I can't stand the pain. I plead, kill me.'

"And I said," the soldier continued, "'Jupiter forgive me,' and I slit my brother's throat. Now do you see why I want to burn to death inside their Temple those disgusting barbarians. Please, let me throw a torch through the window."

I stood there looking at his somber grimy face. All of a sudden flashed through my mind the image of my youthful comrade, Antonio Julius Lepidus, gory head severed from his body, my best friend killed as was this man's brother.

"I am going away," I said, turning my horse's head. "I saw nothing. Do what you want."

A cheer came up from the massed legionnaires. I trotted through the debris, not looking back. As I rode down the slope from the Temple, I saw two soldiers, tin water cups in hand, trying to catch some of the molten gold and silver flowing from the plates over the burning gates that my father had donated.

XXI

The rebellion was over. The butchery had ceased. Two fortresses still were unconquered in the desert to the south, Herodium and Masada, but they were of little importance and would be taken at our leisure. Judaea for all intents and purposes as the homeland of the Judeans no longer existed, what with the slaughter in the north by Vespasian during the earlier period and the conquest of Jerusalem.

Josephus tried to make a census of the losses. He calculated that before the siege of Jerusalem almost two million persons were killed in the north and adjacent areas. At Jerusalem the captives sold as slaves were about 97,000 while those killed during the siege ran from 600,000 to 1,100,000, the city's population having been enormously bloated due to the Passover holiday inflow from other countries and the refugees escaping from Vespasian's conquest of the rest of the province. Many captives were killed soon after as unwilling gladiators at Caesarea and Rome; many others perished working in the mines.

I myself felt that Josephus's estimates were swelled to please Titus since before the revolt the entire population of Judaea had been considered as some 2,500,000, and even including the inflow into Jerusalem from elsewhere the figures seemed much too high. But there was no question that the Judean land, to be sold to speculators or settled by retired legionnaires, would lead to a province inhabited by the Jews as a minority. It was also a fact that the gold ransacked from the Temple was so great its price dropped by half on the Syrian market, as did the cost of slaves.

It had always seemed to me that the war in Judaea was also exaggerated in importance by Josephus to ingratiate himself with Vespasian and Titus in order to give strength and legitimacy to their taking of power after a century of rule by the Julio-Claudians. Vespasian needed to consolidate his reign by a great Roman victory and such a victory and subsequent Triumph parade were essential to his credibility as an upstart emperor. For example, Divus Augustus lost three entire legions, some 20,000 men in the battle at Teutoburg in Germania. And even the violent fight for supreme power between Vitellius and Vespasian was claimed to have led to the slaughter of an enormous number of legionnaires. To the contrary, the Roman losses at Jerusalem were meager and included as well allied troops who were not legionnaires. It was thus to Vespasian's advantage to have the victory presented as extraordinary, particularly under the martial skill of his son Titus while in reality the Judean campaign was merely one of the many mutinies against Rome since its dominance and a piddling affair compared to the three Punic Wars against Carthage.

As to the three walls surrounding Jerusalem the first was thickest and took fifteen days to break through. The second, though at first obstinate, was broken through in five days. The third was undermined and collapsed. The conquest thus was swift. It was the fanaticism of the defenders as well that magnified the victory. In Germania, after losing pitched battles the defeated would simply disappear into the dense forests. In fights between legions the beaten troops were often incorporated into those of the victor: the fighting was done for money, not principle. In Jerusalem the defenders seemed to have no regard for their lives and would, though not trained soldiers, often defeat in direct combat the legionnaires who were astonished by their reckless courage.

Another factor was that Josephus, now given by Vespasian his family name of Flavius as we received the name Julius from Divus

Augustus, wrote about the war in detail to magnify not only its significance and the heroism and humanity of Titus, but to advance himself personally. In that he was successful, receiving large land grants and a fine pension. I heard later from Princess Berenice that before publishing his work on the Judean war he submitted it for approval to both Vespasian and Titus. Under those circumstances he would naturally magnify their strengths and virtues.

As to the destruction of the Temple, though not deliberate, it was a typical act in total war. The Romans indeed went further in their conflicts with Carthage and Corinth, completely destroying the cities and plowing over the debris. The wreckage at Jerusalem and the destruction of their Temple meant much to the Judeans, but they were not a very significant group in the Roman Empire and no longer had to be favored now that peace with Parthia seemed sure.

Speaking for myself as a born Jew in Egypt, whose father had contributed the gold and silver plating over the nine gates of the Temple, I did have mixed feelings about those events but they did not distract me from my duty as a Roman commander. Judaea was a Roman province in revolt; therefore its submission was necessary. I may add this attitude was shared by King Agrippa II and his sister Princess Berenice, the mistress of Titus. It was also shared by many of the Judean nobility and high-standing rabbis, who condemned the Zealots dominating Jerusalem—and who, deserters claimed, often broke the scriptural injunctions. These rabbis clearly distinguished their religion from the province that had rebelled. Even from a practical point of view there were as many Jews living in Alexandria at the outbreak of the revolt as there were in Jerusalem, so destruction of the religion was not involved.

To sum up. I might conclude with more than a touch of irony that without Josephus taking copious notes intending to write a book on the events, and also to flatter Titus and Vespasian and ingratiate himself for personal gain, the war would have been a minor episode in Roman history. One might say it was unfortunate for the Carthaginians that they didn't have a Josephus!

It was a cloudy day as I sat on my horse looking at the ruins of Jerusalem, reflecting on the devastation with odd feelings, when Titus came riding up dressed in his cuirass and red coat. "Well, we did it, *Actua est fabula*; it's over," he said cheerfully, not bothered at all by the carnage.

"And you will get your Triumph in Rome, which you amply deserve," I said.

"Tiberius, I have good news for you," Titus said.

"Oh?" I asked.

"I wrote my father how greatly you helped me, having served as our procurator in Judaea many years ago and knowing the language. It is true; and my father wrote back that he decided to make you his *praefectus praetorio*, commander of the praetorian guard. As you know, after the emperor and of course myself and my brother Domitian, that is the highest post in the empire because on the praefectus rests the security of the emperor. Divus Caligula and Divus Nero were both deserted by them, which led to their deaths. My father wrote that he has more confidence in your integrity than anyone else in the empire, so he wants you to be responsible for his security."

"By Jupiter!" I exclaimed. "What an honor. You're not joking?" I knew Titus's sense of humor.

"I don't joke in such matters," Titus said. "You've done a great job. Congratulations." He laughed. "Judaea is now a land cleansed of its people. No more revolts here, though with these imbeciles, reduced as they are, you never can tell." And he wheeled his horse, smiled, shook his head in farewell, and was off.

For most of the four months of the siege the sky had been clear over Jerusalem except for a very bright star that seemed to some as though in the form of a sword: I myself noted it. Then in the last week during our final assault the heavens darkened and we were lashed by thunder and lightning. As Titus left, a vivid flash lit the sky. I felt a violent shock and my body trembled.

I fell from my horse and lay as dead. "I've been hit by lightning." I thought at that last moment and out of my remote childhood I saw my father at the dinner table, standing and reciting *Akoue, Israel! Kyrios, ho Theos hêmon, kyrios heis estin.* "Hear, O Israel: the Lord our God is one Lord."

Miraculously the fall was not fatal, though as I look back I wish it had been. I was so inert that the shock of falling broke no bones. I was taken to my private quarters and told I raved in Greek for several days. Then I recovered.

It must have been at least five days later when I again attended the daily War Council. I was met with great pleasure by the commanders, who had obviously been told by Titus of my proposed elevation to be *praefectus praetorio* at Rome; and as I reflected to myself with some wryness, their affectionate greetings involved self-interest, for no friend of the head of the praetorian guard feared his post or being compelled to commit suicide.

"You missed the fun," said Marcus Antonius Julianus, our newest procurator of Judaea and member of the Council.

"What fun?"

"We were all curious as to what it was like in their inner sanctum, the mysterious last room at the top of the Temple where their Yahweh was supposed to live. When we finally killed off the Temple defenders—they refused to surrender—Titus, with Commander Fronto and me, decided once and for all to find out what those maniacs were fighting for. At the top was a long gallery paneled with cedar and cypress wood, leading off to various rooms. At the end of the corridor there was a large curtain dividing two rooms, a beautiful curtain by the way, embroidered with blue lines as well as scarlet and purple. Titus told his accompanying legionnaires to pull it down carefully and fold it up."

I glanced at Titus. He winked at me. I knew where the curtain was headed, namely a gift to adorn the bed, a gift to her, where he slept with Princess Berenice.

Julianus continued. "The room before the curtain, we knew, had contained the large seven-branch candlestick and the gold incense container—I say contained because several days ago a high Temple official brought them to us in exchange for his life. Lined up before the entrance to the last room stood about twenty priests, unarmed and chanting some mumbo-jumbo in a monotonous tone. Since I knew some Aramaic as procurator of Judaea," Julianus said, "I ordered them to get away. But with arms folded they stood blocking our entry until Titus, annoyed, motioned to our legionnaires to slit their throats. This they did with no resistance from the priests, who simply fell to the floor while still mumbling what seemed to be their death chant.

"That last room behind the curtain," Julianus said, "I recalled from their customs as Judean procurator was what they called the *Haqadosh haqadoshim*, translated as the Holy of Holies, the room into which once a year, called their Day of Atonement, the high priest would enter and place the incense.

"Titus, always fearless, entered the room first. It was so dark and mysterious, as he can tell you, that he drew his sword. Then his eyes adjusted and he saw . . ."

Fronto, along with Titus and Julianus, burst out laughing. "Titus, tell Tiberius what you saw."

Titus laughed again. "I saw . . . I saw nothing. Absolutely nothing. The room was empty."

"Not quite empty," Fronto added. "There was a rock sticking up in the center of the room. Titus, thinking it might have been a magical rock, perhaps their deity, struck it hard with his sword. A few chips jumped off at the impact. I couldn't help saying to Titus, 'No angel of their Yahweh stopped us!'

"The rock was nothing but the topmost point of the hill on which the Temple was built. A common rock!"

"Can you imagine?" exclaimed Titus. "These idiots are fighting for . . . for nothing. They are atheists. At least we who believe in Jupiter have his image in statues at our holy places and even in the streets. The Greeks also have their Zeus, which is simply another name for Jupiter. But those stupid fools don't even worship an ass's head as some claim. They worship, they die for . . . nothing. They have no God. What do you think of that, Tiberius? Isn't that imbecilic!"

I didn't know what to say. Then I thought of a good answer. "I know nothing of that room. I wasn't there. But I do swear to the coming divinity of the emperor, your father, Emperor Vespasian. That's good enough for me. *Vivat Vespasian* and his sons."

"*Vivat, vivat Vespasian!*" exclaimed the commanders together while Titus smiled in joy.

XXII

A deserter identified Avraharn Moshe, the leading wine merchant of Jerusalem. We asked where was located his underground vaults for storing wine. He refused to say. After chopping off his fingers one by one, with the loss of three he changed his mind and told us. Rather elderly and with a mutilated hand, he wouldn't bring any bids in the slave mart so we slit his throat.

What a hoard! The long vault was so deeply cut below the floor level that the wine bottles had not been affected by the heat of the burning city. Thousands of bottles were stacked at a 45° angle on three groups of shelves, all marked with the places they came from. In one corner there was a separate bin marked *Temed* in Hebrew, signifying the best quality of wine, so we were told.

Titus assigned a trusty centurion to direct a group of prisoners to cart and bring up the bottles to our headquarters. Then, putting aside the *Temed* wine, he declared a holiday for three days after the last rebels were rounded up and invited all the soldiers, including the auxiliary troops (except those of King Agrippa II's forces who had already left for home) to a victory celebration.

It was a debauchery in which, though still feeling unwell, I watched. Several hundred of the best-looking girls had been picked out from the prisoners for the occasion, and they were repeatedly raped by the drunken men. Two of the girls seized daggers from drunks and drove them into their hearts, which amused rather than aroused pity in the legionnaires. Indeed, one soldier, to the cheers of his comrades, fucked one of the corpses, his chest splashed red from her blood. By dawn the large space looked like a battlefield of the dead rather than a celebration, and there was little left to the large hoard of wine.

Our separate celebration was restricted to the commanders, the centurions, the leaders of the auxiliary forces from Parthia, Nabatea, and volunteers from the cities of the Decapolis and the client states of Graecia and Lesser Armenia. It was a more intimate and less rowdy party. The *Temed* wine was reserved for us and delicacies had been specially ordered from a distance. As I thought, Titus had been telling everyone that Emperor Vespasian was going to make me *praefectus praetorio*, and I was overwhelmed with compliments.

A fellow commander who served under me in the Parthian campaign, and with whom therefore I had a more intimate relation, congratulated me fervently and then, eyeing me closely said, "Tiberius my friend, what is that dark red lesion on your cheek? It has grown in size the last few weeks. You ought to have one of our skilled Greek doctors look at it."

"That large red spot?" I asked.

"Yes" he said. It's probably a scab from this filth we live in from those damn rebels."

"I guess I should, though it doesn't hurt," I said.

"We need you too much to have you sick. We settle one problem and another comes along. Thank Jupiter that the Parthians didn't rise up and join the Judeans but stuck to their pact with us or we really would have been in trouble. But now my wife writes that there's a problem again with the Gauls. One thing after another."

XXIII

At this point there was the second split of the parchment scroll. It did not seem serious because the remaining section was smaller than the part I had already translated.

I sighed. The story was fascinating—I felt like I was raising someone from the dead—and wanted to continue. But it was very late and gold spots flickered before my tired eyes. I decided to stop and pick it up tomorrow. Father Hieronymos, after the many summers I spent cataloguing the library, had already told me where I could sleep, sleep indeed later than the monks, who rose early for the morning mass. I even knew where the kitchen was in which I could get a simple but hearty breakfast with Turkish coffee, which, if not diluted, was strong enough to wake the dead.

I stumbled to my cot, tiptoeing past the sleeping monks and, without undressing, threw myself down. But though exhausted, sleep would not come. My work was like an engaging detective novel, though I was translating a true-life drama. It kept drumming through my mind. Where was Morpheus, god of dreams and son of Sleep? I was sure Morpheus was a Greek, or was it a Roman god? I cursed myself. In my youth I had a wonderful memory but now here and there I couldn't think of the words, telephone numbers, or names of acquaintances that would have hopped into my head even ten years ago. Cursing myself seemed to bring Morpheus, for I finally slept.

It must have been seven o'clock when I awoke. The monks were already back from mass, had breakfast and resumed their normal activities. I got up, dressed, went through a quick washing—the hot water at St. Catherine's monastery had never worked well—ate, and returned to the long table on which laid the scroll.

At the edge of the table Father Hieronymos, whose humor at times could be a bit caustic, had left a note: *Ioudaios ton apo Alexandreias*, that is in Greek, "One of the Jews from Alexandria." It was meant kindly, though facetious, and I could not help reflecting that with all our culture, and the fact that the monks knew of my sympathy and even admiration for their vocation, I was not one of them. Even Father Hieronymos!

Back to work. I picked up the remaining piece of the scroll and continued to translate.

"You know," Dr. Discorides said, the famous Greek doctor, "as the basis for my book *Materia Medicina* I studied medicine in Alexandria, which has better medical academies than those of Rome or Athens. I was there several years. I've heard a rumor that you are Greek by origin, which seems to make sense with your name. Have you ever been to the famous temple of the Jews there? They call it a *proseuche*."

"Yes," I said a bit curtly.

"It was an interesting experience. I went out of curiosity. They read their services in Greek, not Aramaic or Hebrew, though I can't tell the difference. The part I could hear, not sitting close in that enormous interior, was from their holy book, the section describing their animal sacrifices. A most barbarous people."

I said nothing. I had long learned in such matters to keep my mouth shut. As the folk proverb goes, "A closed mouth doesn't catch flies."

"Then I decided to read their holy book, called the Pentateuch.

What a mishmash! As a scientist I was amused at the internal contradiction among the five books—there are five, as the name Pentateuch indicates—such as the time difference between Abraham their patriarch and their Joseph in Egypt, or the nonsense of the parting of the Red Sea waters, with the water closing and drowning their pursuers. Or their ridiculous high number of slaves escaping into the Sinai Desert and wandering there for forty years, a sandy waste that could hardly support a lizard."

Dr. Discorides warmed to his subject. As I was silent he thought I didn't know what he was talking about. It was obvious to me as well he seemed hesitant to discuss what my red lesion meant.

"Most of all," he continued, "I came to the conclusion that their Moshe may never have existed or if he did he was probably in rebellion against the reigning pharaoh and headed a slave insurrection. I had also studied Egyptian history at Alexandria. The name Moshe or Mose, separately or part of a larger one, is aristocratic, that of a royal line of pharaohs, namely Thutmose I through Thutmose IV. There was even a famous scribe in the reign of Ramses II with that name, which puts their Moshe or Mose close to the time they claim he lived. What makes the fable more understandable, according to what I read at the Great Library in Alexandria, is that the Egyptian Mose, or Mes in this case, was originally the son of one of the Egyptian gods, closer to what the Jews believe." He laughed. "Maybe their sort of deity was a very early aristocratic Spartacus."

I could no longer hold my tongue. What the doctor was saying sounded too much like my adolescent thoughts, and indeed conversations, with my father and Uncle Philo. Besides, I must admit that something in my religious training resented what the learned doctor was saying, and what I believed myself. I had evaded such thoughts for many years because they brought back buried memories of my youth.

I knew these Greeks revered their own ancient past. I would be careful, but why not give Dr. Discorides a taste of his own medicine, so to speak?

"And if you will excuse me," I said, "speaking as a Roman, how is that any different from the esteemed Greek stories, which might be considered as mythical as the Judean ones. Did Homer exist? What is the evidence? Did the Greeks go into a long war simply over the ravishing of a woman, Helena? After all, the Greeks thought as little of women as do these Judeans. Most likely, given the strategic position of Troy at the mouth of the Black Sea, it was a fight over control of trade routes and the poet or poets justified the war by that story. Remember the adventures told in the Odyssey! Have you ever seen a Cyclops, for example? Most of all, that ridiculous background of the gods being split in the Trojan War, some favoring one side and some the other!"

"I see you know our literature," Dr. Discorides said wryly.

"I too, though a military man, have some education. In fact, I was born in Alexandria and went to the top Greek academy there, though my family was Julio-Claudian."

I was a bit irritated. "All people have myths as to their origins, the Judeans, the Greeks, even the Romans. We have Romulus and Remus, twin sons of Mars, suckled by a she-wolf, the founders of our great city. These myths are like glue holding the papyrus sheets together to make a book. The Judeans are no better or worse than other peoples; they indeed like the Romans and Greeks held and still hold a conviction they are superior to others. The problem with the Judeans is that they have converted this conviction into some kind of divine link to their Yahweh, Jupiter to us Romans, Zeus to you Greeks. I know; I served as procurator in Judaea many years ago. Most of them are convinced with absolute crazy fanaticism that they are the Chosen People destined to convert the world to their Yahweh. There is even a new sect among them which claims they have given birth to what they call a Messiah, an Anointed One, some say even a son of their God sent now to convert the world."

"Sounds a bit like Caligula," laughed Dr. Discorides.

"Very much so except their so-called Messiah, who was incidentally crucified about forty years ago for arousing civil discord in

Jerusalem, preached peace rather than war and humility rather than arrogance."

"Are you one of his followers?" asked the doctor with a twinkle in his eyes.

"Peace! With me! I believe, as should a Roman commander, in war, those wars that bring Roman civilization to backward and barbarous peoples; and which I may add where we have absorbed with gratitude Greek art, architecture, and literature."

Dr. Discorides smiled. "We are now in complete agreement. But tell me, unfortunately getting back the reason I am here, how could a high Roman commander like you with no or minimal contact with common people get a grave disease?"

Now at last we were getting to the point. A shiver went down my back.

"What grave disease?" I asked.

"I dislike what I have to say but I must. It is Elephantiasis Graecorum, or leprosy as it is commonly called."

I slumped in my chair. My mind went blank. I swallowed and then shuddered. "Are you sure?"

"Yes," Dr. Discorides said. "There is no doubt. How could that happen to you?"

"I have no idea." My mind awakened, started to whirl.

"It is a curious thing," the doctor said, maintaining a careful objective attitude, "I told you that I have read Judean so-called sacred literature, as I do the literature of other barbarous people, and was struck by an oddity. These totally unscientific people had in one part of their literature an almost Greek analysis, and that was on the very subject of leprosy. It is in their book called Leviticus, when their Moshe and his brother Aharon received from their Yahweh a message describing leprosy and how to distinguish it from mere scabs. It is, I repeat, quite scientific, amazingly so from such a backward culture!"

My mind was not on his words.

"Wait!" I said with agitation. "Now I may have the answer. As I mentioned, I was a procurator of Judaea many years ago. I had visited King Agrippa II at his kingdom in the Galilee and riding back to Jerusalem a group of lepers came toward the road, hands outstretched, begging alms. I was told they used to isolate lepers but no more. They were horrible, without fingers or had stumps for arms, some so-called lion faces distorted by the disease. They called out Unclean, Unclean—I still remember the word in their language, *Amê, Amê*—which is the law, for they would be put to death without that warning.

"One of them caught my attention and I gasped. Despite the distortion of his face he looked very much like my long-dead brother Marcus. I pulled the reins of my horse and dismounted. 'Careful. Don't go too near,' cautioned one of my guards. I stopped and looked more carefully at that leper. Noticing my attention he smiled in a ghastly way, walked toward me, and extended his hand for alms.

"Careful," the guard warned me again.

"I motioned to the leper to stop and he did, still with that horrible smile.

"I hadn't been mistaken. He looked so much like my poor dead brother I almost fainted. Reaching into my pocket I drew out four aureii—which for him was an enormous sum of gold—and threw it at his feet. He smiled again, I could swear almost slyly, picked up the money, and walked back to the other lepers."

"How far away from him were you?" asked Dr. Discorides.

"Perhaps five paces."

"That's it of course. He gave you the disease."

"But that's ridiculous. I never touched him."

"You don't have to. We've learned that leprosy is only very contagious in early years but the breath of a leper in that period can pass the disease."

I sank back. "It was about twenty years ago. How long do I have?"

Dr. Discorides avoided my eyes. "Perhaps five years," he said. "The total progress of leprosy can run more than twenty years. The end period, however, is very difficult. There are stoics who solve their problem before that, if you know what I mean."

"Thank you, doctor," I said. "Then from what you tell me there is no remedy."

"None."

"Thank you again," I said. "Now I would like to be left alone with my thoughts."

"I understand," he said, and left.

My first impulse was to go to the closet containing my dagger and plunge it into my heart. I was not afraid of death. I had faced it several times. Then a peculiar memory crossed my mind and I almost laughed. I recalled again how Emperor Claudius, when learning of the orgies of his wife Messalina, had ordered her to commit suicide. She was with her mother Domitia Lepida when receiving the news. Messalina put a dagger to her throat and then to her breast, but couldn't drive it in. Her mother was reputed to have said, "It won't hurt you if you drive it in quickly." Hesitating, an officer of the praetorian guard entered and stabbed Messalina to death.

This story became folklore among the high Roman nobility who were often ordered to commit suicide by Nero: the soldiers sent to check those reluctant were reputed to quote the phrase with irony, "It won't hurt if you drive it in quickly."

I put down my dagger and thought of the luck of my dear friend Antonio Julius Lepidus, who died the way I would have liked to die. I even thought of deliberately approaching close to the last besieged Judean rebels in one of their two desert fortresses, to be killed by a dart and join Antonio—where? But my thoughts kept swinging over and over to that leper who looked like my brother Marcus and that curious sly look on his face as he picked up the gold.

It struck me with full force, as the same thought had entered my mind after I ordered the putting down of the Jewish insurrection in Alexandria which led to the death of my mother. There had been a continuity in my life. It was not my extraordinary advance to the top-most level of the Roman military, though admittedly it seems a miracle for a born Egyptian, not to mention one born in my religion. It was that my rise appeared to be the touch of death. Everyone dear to me had died. Since deliberately forsaking my family and my religious community my touch seemed fatal. Was that leper, who looked so much like my brother Marcus, sent by Yahweh to destroy me slowly and in great pain?

"Nonsense," I said out loud. "Nonsense," I shrieked and banged my head against the table as, when a boy, I had seen an old Jew do that against the seat before him in the Alexandrian *proseuche* while standing to recite the Kaddish or death prayer for some beloved person.

My head hurt. I reached to the other side of the table where stood a bottle of wine, poured out a glass, and said to myself in a softer tone, "Nonsense. You are not superstitious. You don't believe in ghosts or spirits or resurrection. You are in a way like those Sadducees in Judaea who came over to our side and disbelieve in such spiritual nonsense. Accept! Accept what fate ordains, good or bad, and accept to the end your destiny. *Tempus abire tibi est*, your time is up. You have been very lucky. Now you are unlucky. That is all."

The next morning I received a note from Titus:

> Commander Tiberius. My dear general and friend, I would appreciate your not coming to the next Council meeting nor indeed to any others. I have spoken to Dr. Discorides. What can I add? We both as Romans know our duty. I am arranging a comfortable life for you near the city of Tiberius on a confiscated large estate overlooking the Sea of Galilee, as well as providing two dozen Greek slaves to care for you. Exact instructions as to the details will be sent to you.
>
> I can only state *ab imo pectore*; from my head as well as my heart, good luck. You are, were, and will remain a great credit to our Roman nobility.
>
> Your friend, Titus.

I grimaced. Roman nobility! I, a Jew from Alexandria, had played the game and played it well, fooling almost everyone but myself. And perhaps Yahweh, if He is. My father's Greek prayer when I was a boy, after blessing the bread before meals, came back to me again, the second time in weeks: *Akoue, Israel! Kyrios, he Theos hêmon, kyrios heis estin.* The tears came to my eyes. "Forgive me father. I knew not what I did." Then I straightened up in my chair and drank another glass of wine. I blew out the oil lamp's flaming wick and threw myself on the military couch.

XXIV

The estate was indeed large, on a hillock overlooking the city of Tiberius ("how ironic," I thought) and the Jordan Valley. Titus, always shrewd, had provided me solely with Greek slaves, knowing full well that any Jew would have murdered me. One of the Greeks, Isocrates, who came from the Ionian islands, was clever, well educated, and, repeating myself, became my scribe. I promised him his freedom on my death. He continues to write these notes as I dictate.

The first two years I could still read. I went back to the Egyptian Jewish folktales told me as a child: Artapanos, a historical novel about Moses and Joseph; the love story called Joseph and Asenath, touching in its naiveté; and of course the dialogues of my Uncle Philo, which I confess bored me. Then I read again the Greek immortals whose writings I had studied in my youth at the Alexandrian academy: Aristotle, Plato, Plutarch, Thucydides. But I soon realized that an old mind is no longer as open and inquisitive as a young mind, and I often found myself dozing while reading those geniuses. I began to find it more interesting to review with older and wiser eyes the Pentateuch and other Jewish sacred writings. My father had compelled me to study them from infancy so I knew them quite well. A story that involved me was how King Uzzia of Judaea, who lived only a few hundred years after kings David and Solomon, had leprosy, was isolated, and was even given a separate burial. If they had continued to isolate lepers in our time, I thought bitterly, I wouldn't be stuck on a hilltop in Galilee but rather would hold the post of *praefectus praetorio* for Emperor Vespasian, the most important man in the Roman Empire after the imperial family.

In the Judean *Second Book of Kings* there is told another interesting story. Naaman, a general of the Syrian army, was also a leper. A captured Judean maid in the time of King Jehoram told Naaman's wife that the prophet Elisha could cure his leprosy if he dipped himself in the Jordan River seven times, "and his flesh came again like the flesh of a little child, and he was clean."

What nonsense, I thought.

Lying sleepless two nights later I rang the night bell. A sleepy slave approached. "Get out my mobile chair. I want to go down to the Jordan River."

The slave looked at me as though I had lost my mind but, rousing several other slaves, they lifted me into my chair and in the clear moonlight rolled me to the Jordan River edge. There was a vast silence; not even a dog barked.

"Dump me into the river seven times. Fully with only my nose above the water. Seven times."

"Master, may I inquire why? You could get a bad chill," Isocrates said. He had risen to accompany me.

"Seven times," I said furiously, thinking what an idiot I was.

Seven times they did, following my instructions, and then wrapped in blankets they carried me back to the house.

Of course my flesh did not "come again like the flesh of a little child," and I cursed myself for lapsing into such superstition. It was indeed *aegri somnia*, a sick man's hallucination.

Generally, the seasons went by with unchanging events as I decayed. But I dreaded the nights because of two recurring dreams. At the *proseuch* of Alexandria at the seat of Moses were crouched on either side large stone lions, the lions of Judah, with menacing open jaws and long tails. As a child I sat on a purple silk pillow below my father's chair, next to the seat of Moses. I had this dream. Out of the burning Temple in Jerusalem sprang one of those lions, snarling, large teeth bared, with rigid tail. But his tail was a cross and on the cross I was crucified, with the spikes being the wood roller ends of a Torah scroll. I was screaming in agony, my palms and ankles dripping blood that oozed over the ends of my father's prayer shawl. I cried out, "Father, Father, help me," but he shook off the blood angrily, scowled at me, and turned back to his scriptural reading.

I then would wake up thrashing in my bed.

The second dream was even stranger. When awake I often thought of the remark the old servant Jeremiah had made when Penelope visited our family mansion, namely that my father's eyes had flickered to her enlarged stomach. And also that my agent Solon, when visiting the Philip bookstore, had noticed that Penelope's oldest child was different from the other two children, with dark skin and a somewhat hooked nose.

In my dream the child, named Tiberius, had been brought up by Philip, Penelope's husband, to hate Jews. The boy became a leader of Greek anti-Jewish hoodlums. When as governor I suppressed the Alexandrian riots, which involved sacking the Jewish quarter, young Tiberius in this dream led his gang to our family mansion and killed my father.

After this dream I would wake up smiling. And then, conscious of what the dream implied, I would try to erase it from my mind.

It is three years now here and I can no longer hold a scroll to read. Isocrates, my scribe, reads to me. But I have become bored hearing the same philosophy, the same history, the same poetry. I told Isocrates no more; I prefer to doze in the sunlight. Though leprosy is a hideous disease, it is not painful as the toes, the fingers, and limbs lose sensation, atrophy, and start to drop off.

The first year at my hilltop home I received quite a bit of mail, though of course they all cautioned me to respond only in scrolls that I dictated but did not touch. Titus was quite genteel; he wrote about the activities of the imperial court and how he and his father Vespasian for absolute security had decided to make him *praefectus praetorio* so no fate such as those of Caligula and Nero could occur.

I for one was delighted and wrote him so since, unlike most of the other emperors, Emperor Vespasian thus showed full confidence in his own son. In the second year the scrolls became fewer and fewer, until the only one I received in my third year was on my birthday: Titus retained his remarkable memory for small detail. Now at the end of my third year, no longer anything.

I don't blame Titus. As heir apparent to become emperor of Rome, which Vespasian has openly proclaimed on the reverse of his coinage, he has more to do than write to a dying leper.

From King Agrippa II I heard nothing. He was always a sycophant and only concerned with keeping his small kingdom. A harmless supporter, Vespasian left him in control, probably at the instigation of his son Titus, who was grateful for Agrippa's military support against his fellow Judeans in the Jewish War.

The sole person who kept up a flow of correspondence, and it did not surprise me, was Princess Berenice. Women, I had discovered long before, are usually more gracious and warmer than men, probably due to biology as the bearers of helpless infants. Berenice wrote that she had accompanied her lover Titus back to Rome with the thought he would marry her. She claimed Titus wanted to but his father Vespasian and the Imperial Council violently objected to an Oriental empress and a religious Judean at that. Finally Berenice and Titus had parted reluctantly, and she returned to live with her brother King Agrippa II. Actually, Berenice wrote me recently that Agrippa and she left his capital at Caesarea Philippi and came to pass a few weeks at Tiberius, no more than a few kilometers from me, and that once she had walked to the city's edge and looked up to the hillock on which my property was located and even thought of visiting me. But, she continued, some of the city people who supplied my staff described my unhappy condition and that I would understand. I did. Then that correspondence dwindled as well. It was indeed better that she had not come. Not only was I starting to lose my fingers and toes but my face skin was covered with thick red patches and with open sores, my nose had thickened, its tip lost, and mucus flowed without cease from the holes which had been the nostrils.

I was not lonely nor am I referring to my slaves even though somehow they must have learned that leprosy in its last stages is no longer contagious so they had no fear coming near. I was not lonely for another reason. For the first time in my life I had no duty, no responsibility, no need to push forward my career no matter what or whom I hurt in the process. At last I was free of ambition, free of my mask falling away, and could see the world not through greed of fame but objectively, like those old men I used to observe dozing in the sunlight on the public park benches in Rome and Alexandria. Dying, I was free for the first time.

As I believe I mentioned, through a skilled carpenter down in Tiberius I had one of my slaves arrange a special chair on wheels with handles that could swivel the chair's position and set it up and down. I still had enough control over one hand to manipulate the handles. I would then order a slave to wheel me to a flat spot on the sloping green lawn. The Galilee has very good weather and I would spend most of my time in this chair, nodding, dreaming, sleeping. Once I even thought with irony that getting leprosy in old age was probably better than being head of the praetorian guard protecting the emperor.

It was then I became interested in insects. An ant's nest was situated in the rotting roots of an old tree long since cut down. I remembered dimly there was a queen, or was it a king—I forget which, who lorded over the hive. She or he was fed by slave ants who were kept and "milked" for food. The nest was protected by guards and worker ants foraged for prey.

I decided to write to the Great Library at Alexandria for any work they still had on the subject, stating I had a vague memory of a study which I had read as a student.

The reply was quick. The rector, Professor Diodorus—an Ionian by origin, not a Macedonian as I recalled—wrote that he was delighted to hear from me, the former *praefectus Alexandreae et Aegyptus* and distinguished commander in putting down the insolent

Jews. The quick response amazed me for as a friend and contemporary of my Uncle Philo, who died quite old in the last years of Divus Claudius's reign, Professor Diodorus must have been very advanced in age. His memory was also amazing for he reminded me that the Great Library would be eternally grateful for my doubling their subsidiary when I was Egyptian governor. He wrote that at a recent meeting of the library board it was almost unanimously decided—a few violent Greek nationalists dissenting—to erect marble statues of my Uncle Philo and of me in the hall of the library entrance, thus grouping us with the statues there of the famous Greek philosophers.

As to my specific request Professor Diodorus wrote he could not offhand remember such a study of what he called "social insects" but that he would arrange for several of the librarians to check for such a work. He ended—he must have heard that I was now a leper—that he prayed, though somewhat of an unbeliever, that Zeus would perform a miracle and cure me.

I waited impatiently, wheeling my mobile chair daily to the tree stump containing the ant nest, watching with fascination their activities and dictating these thoughts to my scribe.

About a month later I received an answer from Alexandria. After a close search of the library registry they had discovered a manuscript written by an obscure writer, Nicodemus of Syracusae, who was writing about the time Plato went to that city. Diodorus was having it transcribed and I would receive the work shortly. I wrote back thanking him for the statues and stating, which was true, that doubling the subsidy for the Alexandrian Great Library when I was praefectus of Egypt was one of the things I felt best about doing in my long career. In a short time I received the insect study. It consisted not only of research on ants but bees and wasps as well. Flipping over the pages I had Isocrates cross out many, for the author stated that different varieties of ants lived in different temperature zones and I was only interested in ours.

I admired the writer, this Nicodemus, living so long ago, forgotten, and yet with such keen insight into what he called the social insects.

From my own observations ants were social in one sense but violent warriors in another. The kind I was observing were called wood ants because, as I had noted, they built their nests around and under dead tree stumps. According to Nicodemus they dig chambers into the rotted wood and in the ground directly underneath, and in the cold of winter they retreat into these chambers.

Ant society, I learned, was strictly demarcated into what we would call clear social class differences. One queen ant rules. Most males are wingless except those allotted by nature to fly and mate with young queens from other colonies. The wingless male ants are workers who not only can run fast but have sharp jaws. Some are unusually large, Nicodemus calling them soldier ants, who guard the worker ants while they seek food. These worker ants appear to communicate with each other by touching antennae and sally forth in groups, working as teams to catch food, which they kill by biting their prey together. They also have slaves, aphids who suck the juice from plants and are in turn not only sucked by the ants but protected by them from predators. Raiding parties of the soldier ants travel in different directions, operating from their nests, overcoming other ant colonies and killing for food the conquered ants as well as crickets, spiders, and centipedes. At the home nest, the wingless females, who do not reproduce, care for the eggs of the queen ant.

Most interesting to me, newly mated queens often start a colony together but as the colony grows, the queens fight until all are killed but one. Then she rules supreme.

Why was I so interested in these ants, I wondered. As I watched worker ants guarded by the larger soldier ants sally forth one day, the answer came in a flash. These ants were no different than the Roman rulers, indeed no different than Alexander in his march east against Darius of Persia or any Nubian king on the war path in Ethiopia. Whether ants or humans we had the same aggressive nature in search for food and conquest of new territory. The instinct to live, to cooperate against the enemy, to enlarge territory, was similar for all life. There were probably a hundred miniature Roman ant empires within my property; they were there before the Macedonians and the Romans, and would probably be there thousands of years after the names of the Roman emperors, who in their besotted egoism called themselves and were called Divi, would only be names in specialized history books, if that.

I couldn't help thinking these thoughts and burst out laughing: Isocrates, taking down the words as I recited them, looked at me as though I had lost the little wits left me in my condition. "Come, worker ant Isocrates," I mumbled. "Ant Tiberius would go inside. It is too hot out here. Let us leave the Roman insects to their antics."

With a strange look Isocrates swiveled my mobile chair and guided me inside to my room. I called for some red wine; I could still drink and feel the effects of wine.

"To Queen Ant Vespasian," I said, lifting the wine glass in salute. My slave said nothing, looking to his shoes at this blasphemy.

Another year has passed. Now I am almost totally without body sensation except that my mind refuses to die. Princess Berenice has written me again. She states contrary to what I thought would happen, the Judean religion did not collapse with the destruction of the Temple but that the rabbis under Yohanan ben Zakkai, whom I remember Titus permitted to leave Jerusalem at the start of the attack on that city, had set up schools with rabbinic teachers who continued to teach the Judaic rites. Now with the Temple destroyed, as well as most of Jerusalem, these schools had transferred their activities north to the Galilee.

Princess Berenice also added a curious fact. The Yeshuites, as a sect now more non-Jewish than before and expanding in numbers, had their so-called Messiah expound one of his most-quoted sermons on the very hillock where I lived. I knew this to be true because one of my more literate slaves, in fact involved in what I might call this new superstition evolving from the Judaic one, found at the crest of the hill above the house, crudely carved on a stone outcropping, the words BEATUS VIR, or "Blessed the Man." He told me from their religious meetings this was a popular phrase from one of the psalms of David, the first lines which were "Blessed the man who fears the Lord, who delights greatly in His commandments." More lunacy to add to the lunacy of the world, I thought.

That the Yeshuites, or now more often called Christianoi after their belief in Cristos, or the Messiah, were expanding surprised me more than the continued vitality of the Jews. I still remembered the place my Uncle Philo took me to when I was young, where the Yeshuite peculiar ceremony seemed such a mishmash of the Jewish religion with the cults of other Oriental religions, particularly that of Osiris, the most popular Egyptian god who died and rose again. In fact, what my Uncle Philo sarcastically remarked had become true, and circumcision for most, according to Princess Berenice, was no longer necessary to their belief.

How could human beings be so naïve, like the Jewish Pharisees or these Christianoi, to think life would be eternal due to a spirit or soul inside the human body which not even the great Greek doctors who specialized in dissecting the dead could locate? Where was this odd object lodged?

Yet at the same time I had lost interest in Greek and Roman writings and preferred that Isocrates read to me from the Pentateuch and the prophets, especially the mystics like Elisha and Jeremiah, whose words had been so drilled into me as a child. I mouthed over and over these lines, from Jeremiah:

> Cursed be the day wherein I was born:
> Let not the day wherein my mother bore me be blessed.
> Cursed be the man who brought tidings to my Father,
> Saying, "A man child is born unto thee,"
> Making him very glad.

I am now close to death. This is the fourth year here and I hardly have any sensation in my body, though I can still dictate my thoughts. I am spoon-fed and water is carefully poured down my throat. There is no point in drinking wine anymore because I feel nothing. But I am not afraid. I am an old wreck of a man who lived gloriously a good part of my life and, still a confirmed epicure, am convinced that there was nothing of me, of the *ego* as the Romans say, before I was born, and that there will be nothing of me after I die. Surely the writings, the literature of geniuses like Thucydides or Aristotle will continue, but of the personal I, nothing. Seek pleasure and avoid pain, as Epicurus wrote. *Carpe diem*; since we must go, seize the day. And yet I admit there are moments when I feel this philosophy is superficial.

I dictated these thoughts in a scroll I sent to Princess Berenice and she in her reply wrote she was very disturbed. Starting her life as an aristocratic Sadducee, whose opinions on human morality were somewhat like mine, as she aged she had become more convinced that there is an afterlife, that the good are rewarded while the bad are condemned in a future existence. She was terrified, she admitted, that Yahweh would send her to Gehenna, the Jewish hell, for her immoral life.

I dictated with difficulty a response, stating she ought not to worry for she tried her best to save the Temple and if Yahweh exists, or if He is, as my father phrased it, He would be compassionate.

Now all has started to darken. My sight, which had been good almost to the end, is leaving. I can hardly swallow the mash fed me and I gag on water spooned down my throat. More and more my thinking returns to early childhood. I can feel my mother kissing me when, afraid of the dark, I crawl into her bed. I hear my father saying, "Rachel, he is a boy now and no longer a baby. Send him back to bed." I feel the hatred I have for him in not letting me cuddle next to my mother.

It gets darker and darker. I no longer can take food or drink. I earlier gave instructions to Isocrates to bring to the Great Library at Alexandria these lifetime musings and, when delivered, he would then be free. This was arranged through a lawyer in Tiberius two years ago.

Why, there is my mother again. She smiles at me. There is my little brother Marcus skipping pebbles with me from the walkway over the waters of the Megas Liman at Alexandria. There is my dear friend Antonio Julius Lepidus mounted on his horse at Rome when we went to cheer for the Green Faction of charioteers. There is . . . I am standing at the railing of the Heptastadium watching the pleasure yachts plying the waters below while the white and grey gulls float overhead. A beautiful girl holds my hand. I feel again that sensation of utter serenity, when I was out of myself and into eternity.

Of course. How stupid of me. I know now the answer. It is simple. The answer, what links these memories together, what is the essence of different religions, is the search for love, that love and its sister kindness, which separate us from the ants or men like Caligula and Nero; though it can be for this or that person or this and that thing, these are curtains behind which is indescribable love itself, a radiant pearl within the husk, the eternal beatitude which binds us together. My life had been built on a lie, the lie of power, that power which corrupts and makes us ugly human beings. The only real truth is love.

I can feel my heart slow. It has grown pitch black. Then whirling up in a hurricane of light there is brilliant luminescence, a white sky of splendor. It dazzles. It beckons.

Why, what is that? Why, there goes the prophet Elijah in a chariot drawn by a whirlwind to heaven by horses of fire. And who is there sitting besides Elijah in that blaze of light? No. Impossible. Yes, it is . . .

XXV

This postscript is by Isocrates, the slave and scribe of the late Commander Tiberius Julius Alexander, found dead yesterday afternoon in his mobile chair with a strange, luminous look on his horribly distorted face.

That luminous smile still confuses me. As he lay dying earlier in the afternoon I tried to get him to swallow some bread dipped in wine. But he was too far gone even to recognize me. I couldn't hear his last mumblings and was curious. What were those last words of this very great man, first epistrategus of southern Egypt, then procurator of Judaea, then praefectus of Alexandria and all Egypt, then top military commander for General Corbulo in the conquest of Greater Armenia as well as under Titus when he destroyed the rebels of Jerusalem. What would be his last words?

I had bent close. There was a name, repeated. I bent still closer. Now I heard. His last words were "Penelope, ah Penelope."

When, as instructed two years before the death of my master, I Isocrates brought to a lawyer in the city of Tiberius his last will and testament, I was not aware that it would be superseded by a new will, written only a few months before his death but giving Princess Berenice full right and authority to execute it.

The new will had many features in common with the older one. It freed all us two dozen slaves, allotting fifty gold aureii to each and two hundred to me—a fortune which will permit me to retire in comfort to the city of Athens after delivering the script to the Great Library in Alexandria.

The provision of the new will which shocked us all was that my master left his house and the rest of his property, of great value, to a certain Yohanan ben Zakkai "to set up another religious school" and there to be taught, as he expressed it, "the fundamental rites of the Judean religion and those most particularly stressing the belief that Yahweh was the essence of love and charity for one's fellow human beings."

We slaves of course had no right to contest any part of the will nor did anyone else for it was sworn to by Princess Berenice, sister of our lord, King Agrippa II. It was so ordered valid and a messenger dispatched to this Yohanan ben Zakkai, located we were told at Yafo, to the south in Judaea on the Great Sea.

My money being held in escrow until the delivery of this long scroll to the rector of the Great Library in Alexandria, I set out. It was an uneventful trip. The rector had already received the news and greeted me politely but with a certain rigid formality; perhaps he had expected a special endowment on my master's death.

Speaking personally, and as a last note, I found Commander Tiberius Julius Alexander a great but strange man full of contradictions, sometimes filled with contempt for men and their ways, especially in religion, and sometimes superstitious to an odd degree. To the end he was proud to belong to the order of *equester ordo*, a Roman knight, and yet full of love for his native city of Alexandria. We, his slaves knew he was born to the Judean religion but thought he was contemptuous of that superstition except in his last two years. At the end, writing to Berenice, he asked me to sign in Greek, possibly in irony, possibly a summing up of his final feelings, *Ioudoios ton apo Alexandreias*, or simply "One of the Jews of Alexandria."

XXVI

It was still dark when I left the monastery, the door clicking shut behind me. I could not see St. Stephen sitting with his staff in a skeleton hand but, passing where I knew he would sit for eternity, I waved. It would probably be for the last time I thought.

The parting, with my manuscript tightly gripped in hand, had been difficult. I had said good-bye after our last supper, affectionately shaking hands with the monks I knew best. The parting with Father Hieronymos had been even more difficult; we were now both old men and the chances were we would never meet again. I fancied I saw a tear in one of his eyes, which he furtively brushed away. I admit I too was so overcome at what was probably our last meeting that I shook his hand and turned away quickly, suppressing a desire to make one final insipid remark.

I stood at the entrance to the monastery and waited for the taxi that Archbishop Demetrios kindly was providing for the trip across the desert to Cairo, where he eagerly awaited the manuscript. It was very early, a faint orange tinge sneaking up the horizon edge to the east over Israel. Soon the earth would be baking in the heat and Archbishop Demetrios, knowing my age, had insisted I leave before the sun rose to great height.

I gazed toward Mt. Sinai, a tall black scar against the grey sky. On its side was a zigzag line of flickering lights, flickering and then dying and flickering again, like fireflies in our American summer. These were the torches of the Moslem pilgrims who had left the large hall next to the mosque where they had briefly stayed before setting out on their pilgrimage to the top of Mt. Sinai. I laughed out loud in the gathering mist of dawn. How Father Hieronymos, forgetting for the moment I was not Greek Orthodox, had grumbled to me about their presence. But they—the Christians—could do nothing. The price of staying in Moslem Egypt had been to accept this Islamic enclave in their monastery.

The dawn light quickened and Mt. Sinai stood out sharper against the sky, huge, ominous, almost gnashing its stone bulk at the world. The flickering torches held by the Moslem pilgrims faded; they must be near the top. Islam, the submission to the will of Allah for Moslems; *Beatus Vir*, the Christian delight in Jehovah's commandments; Moses, the Jewish fear of Yahweh being the start of wisdom. Yahweh and its variants, Allah and Jehovah, all the same God.

From my religious childhood, which I shared with Tiberius Julius Alexander, came back the words from Exodus: And the Lord said to Moses, be ready in the morning and come up to me to the top of the mountain. And Moses rose up early in the morning and went up to Mt. Sinai. And the Lord descended in a cloud and passed by before Moses. And Moses listened to the words of the Lord and he wrote down upon two tables of stones he had brought the words of the Ten Commandments.

It was getting lighter. A few white clouds could now be seen, one in an odd shape crossing Mt. Sinai. Involuntarily I shivered though it was not the early dawn's cool air.

Did we create Him or did He create us? I shivered again, my Epicurean philosophy sliding on soft ground, like that of Tiberius Julius Alexander toward his end. At times, while writing down the story of his life I had felt we were brothers or that he had slipped from his skin into my skin, a passage of souls.

I thought again of those Moslem pilgrims, now at the top of Mt. Sinai, prostrating themselves where the words of Allah had been given to Mohammed through Moses. Those pilgrims believed completely and without the slightest doubt. What was truth? as Pontius Pilate famously asked. And did a fable become true if believed by many millions or was a fable itself the truth like the tortoise within its shell?

My mind was whirling. For a moment, with St. Stephen now revealed in fuller light, I thought he raised his staff to beckon me.

I heard a noise. It was not St. Stephen. It was the approach of the taxi which would take me to Cairo. I grasped the manuscript more firmly. I took a last look at the monastery. Then I thought of Alexander and Darius, my two cats. How they would purr in pleasure on seeing me. It was a comforting thought.

The taxi turned. I took a last look at Mt. Sinai now bathed in light, huge, inscrutable, eternal. I got into the taxi and closed my eyes. A nap would help me regain my philosophical values. I nodded my head and leaned back against the seat. One thought intruded again before I slept.

Did we create Him or did He create us?

The wind whistled through the open window and I seemed to hear a mocking laugh. Then I slept.

www.ingramcontent.com/pod-product-compliance
Lightning Source LLC
Chambersburg PA
CBHW030426310726
48979CB00009B/1639/J

* 9 7 8 1 6 1 6 1 4 1 7 5 2 *